CW00350197

A catalogue record for this book is available from the British Library.

First published in the United Kingdom in 2022 by Peninsula Press

400 Kingsland Road
E8 4AA
London
peninsulapress.co.uk

Cover design by Jo Walker
Typesetting by

Printed in Great Britain by CPI Group (UK) Ltd, Croydon

2 4 6 8 10 9 7 5 3 1
ISBN-13: 9781913512118

The Cellist

Jennifer Atkins

P

PENINSULA PRESS, LONDON

When I first started performing, which was many years ago now, it only seemed to me a question of certainty. I mean making an interpretation, picking an angle, claiming one reading as true over all others. It was about embodying the music, the moment—I couldn't imagine anything bolder than that. I don't know how I came to this view of things, if it was my musical training, or what led me to seek that training in the first place, but interpretation was the path away from doubt, and doubt, for me, was nonexistence. There was no room for doubt on the stage. There could be no room for doubt with my cello. Of course, there was room—once there was, I saw there had only ever been room—but it took me a long time to realise that. It took a whole career to see that doubt, in the end, is what lasts. Doubt, in the end, is the performance.

There is a classical music festival that takes place every autumn in the Midlands, and last month I bumped into a flautist I know on the train there. It was a Friday morning with the country sullen and misty out the windows. She made her way up the carriage just after we'd left London, her flute case strapped across her chest, and I knew she was going to the festival from the stoic look in her eyes and the freshness of her hair cut. I knew as well that she'd feel obliged to sit opposite me, and I had lost the blankness of the journey, which I'd been wanting.

We discussed the programme for the weekend as the train passed open fields and through woods where the trees were nearly leafless, and the mist hung low over the bracken. She kept darting her eyes to my cello case, which was propped against the seat beside me. It was a bulky, silent companion. She had a white silk scarf tied around her hair that was sleek and reminded me of her own instrument. We had studied together at the Academy, and I found myself enjoying our conversation—the flippant way she rolled her eyes as she spoke of her husband, her orchestra—the things I assumed she cared most about.

'I was thinking about you,' she said, 'The other day, I was listening to the Schumann.' She leant her head back on the seat as we entered a tunnel and the lights in the carriage appeared brighter.

I had performed the solo of Schumann's Cello Concerto with the orchestra she played for whilst both of us were in our twenties, and I remembered being terrified to attempt that piece of music, and I recalled too the excitement and hysteria of those years when neither of us had known if we'd make it.

'I was thinking we were wrong,' she said, 'I realised we'd allowed it to become too intimate. But do you remember?'

She went on to describe a distance that had opened up between the string section and me during the concert. She spoke about a particular moment, around halfway through the first movement, and asked if I didn't see that my performance had contained a hardness, which arose from my instrument sounding isolated, because the emotions of the solo couldn't survive all by themselves.

'I remember it sounding as if you didn't believe in it,' she said. 'Like you didn't believe in what the music was doing. I don't know if you wanted to sound like that?'

'Why would I have?'

She had been smiling, but as she realised that I wasn't going to smile, she became more serious.

'Well, there was something untouchable about it, I think.'

She continued looking at me with the same seriousness, and then she turned her attention to the window. The train was moving through what seemed to be a valley, but it was hard to tell through the fog, which was thicker. We were shunted in our seats, and I felt we were barrelling somewhere too fast, yet she was sitting with her back to where we headed, seemingly undaunted. I wondered why she didn't appear more worried. I had no clue what she was trying to tell me. In the reflection of the window, her face took on the qualities of which she'd just spoken, being hard, being impenetrable. We knew things specific to each other, she and I, about the sorts of lives we'd led, the things we'd chosen or discarded, and yet that knowledge never seemed to bring us closer.

Once the train arrived, she told me she had to run, but she hoped I'd be at her performance that evening. I felt disoriented, strangely vicious. She'd been trying to make me surrender to her view of things, and I'd stayed silent, when I should have said if there'd been a problem, *belief* wasn't it. I believe in my instrument in the same way I believe in my own life.

I should have told her that. I knew why I didn't.

That concerto, Schumann's, is seen as the first great cello concerto of the Romantic era. It has three movements, between which Schumann left no gaps—he wanted no opportunity for applause—and the themes throughout repeat and advance, so that the composition is intensely unified. There is almost a sense of endlessness in the repetitions. But, in fact, it is compact, far shorter than other concertos.

Initially, it fell out of the repertoire because of its lack of convention, its oddness. The original manuscript is written obscurely, in a way that makes it challenging to perform—the orchestration is too thin, the tempos are either much too fast, or far too slow. This oddness was taken as evidence of Schumann's mental illness, but it's possible it was just meant to be odd. It hasn't always seemed to me that what is true should be easy to perform. And its strangeness is what has drawn cellists to it, which led, eventually, to its re-emergence, its appreciation.

The specific moment the flautist was talking about is halfway through the first movement, when the opening melody of the cello begins again. It is a reprisal, made more compelling by the fact a false return precedes it—a moment when the opening melody begins but then fades, is not reprised, goes nowhere. The false return cannot be forgotten. And I know why she focused on this point in the music. I, too, have always wanted to know what

Schumann means by it—what exactly we're supposed to gather in this sense of trickery, of falsity, of loss. Because it's painful, really.

I think she was wrong. I did believe in the music. Perhaps I believed in it too much, and I feel ashamed I didn't account for that on the train—that I couldn't tell her just how painful I've found it.

There was a morning, early in our relationship, when Billy asked me to re-string my cello for him. He claimed to be fascinated by the tension. I'd told him it was only tension that kept the different parts of the instrument—the bridge and the strings—together, which allowed for the singularity of the reverberations. He wanted to use the idea in his sculptures, and also, he said, he wanted to watch me do it: the fluency of my fingers, their bold proficiency.

I put my cello on the kitchen table, and he sat with his elbows resting on the surface, instructing me to repeat what I'd done so he could watch again, asking questions to find the reasons behind my actions. He undertook this observation intently, as he did everything, and it was this intentness—how he had the nature of a withdrawn child, standing on the outskirts of a party—that I always found erotic. Similarly, he seemed to enjoy, in those early days, my focus, the lines revealed between my eyebrows when I studied my instrument. Often tasks like this would go on for hours: one of us demonstrating a part of our practice as the other watched, until we ended up in bed together.

Later, he turned me on my belly, wrapped his hands in my dark hair, kissed the birth mark on the soft part of my shoulder. He kissed me there, on that mark of my origin, and the new strings were taut, afterwards, when I played them. They were just like his tongue, is what I remember.

Billy never asked why I chose the cello. That might be the reason I felt, immediately, I could trust him. I never asked why he wanted to be a sculptor either. It was just a fact we lived with desire—we did not feel the need to account for it. I doubt I've ever accounted for my desire. People have asked over the years: why the cello, why specifically, and I've come up with complex answers, or I've said nothing, or I've claimed the only way I can answer is to play, which is half true. I'm not sure I could have said that to him. I believe he would've seen through that. To him, I would've had to say the only real thing I could, which is that my instrument is large, and I was small when I chose it, and it was something—this largeness—which I could hold onto. I needed more than anything to do that.

Before we started dating, he showed up at a recital I gave in Wapping. I was playing for a well-known quartet at the time, which was led by a violinist who'd risen to fame in the nineties, and our events schedule was slowing down for summer. I'd taken a night out of rehearsals to perform with a friend who was a pianist. The tickets had sold out, so we were excited beforehand, the pianist and I, standing in the sunny alley beside the music hall, having a drink and chatting. He mentioned his friend Billy was coming.

'Do you know him? He says you met.'

And we had, sort of, at a party, a few years after I'd graduated. Even though I remembered this, I replied something noncommittal to the pianist, feigning ignorance. An excessive heat had come over me. There was no doubt in my mind about concealing the memory; it would've been impossible to reveal without risking some further exposure. There had been an exchange between Billy and I at that party, which I'd found extremely charged without being able to pinpoint why, and I did not want the pianist to know, and I did not trust myself to speak without betraying the feeling.

We were performing Rachmaninov's Cello Sonata in G Minor, a piece that elevates the piano's role above that of an accompaniment, so my friend might showcase his talent. I had not been nervous of playing this music, but when we eventually walked onto the stage the texture of the evening seemed disrupted. I imagined Billy in the waiting silence, watching with that intentness about him, which I remembered, and I wanted to see again the pink turn of his lips, the clear, grey eyes that rose slightly in the outer corners. But I was also unable to look out to the audience.

I felt afraid of discovery, somehow, of being spotted. Because of this I kept my eyes on the pianist throughout our performance, anticipating and building upon his movements, yet I found my playing was tight and my mind kept edging towards a space at the back of the hall, just before the faces disappeared into darkness. Once the performance was over, when I finally allowed myself to look, Billy was in this space. What sort of perception might that be described as? It was as if I'd looked out and seen him there, watching me, thousands of times. As if it was old ground I was re-treading.

The bar of the music hall was busy after the performance, and he was on the other side of the room talking with people I didn't recognise. I could not stay for more than one drink because I had an early practice, and soon a friend who lived near me asked if I wanted to leave with a few others who were going. I didn't want to leave, although I knew I should, but as we stood there, Billy appeared next to us. He was in a white t-shirt and blue jeans, his body slim beneath them. He asked if we were walking to the station, and so my friend repeated herself.

When I came back outside with my cello, he was standing with my friends, twisting a small silver hoop in his left ear. By that time, it was cooler. I was restless, uncertain if we would have the chance to speak, but as we walked towards the Overground station, he and I came closer together, so that, incrementally, we broke apart from the others. We were walking beside an elevated railway line where once in a while a bright train would pass us. The lights from the carriages illuminated him, briefly, when this happened.

At that party, all those years before, we'd met in a dark bedroom. I'd found him sitting alone on the bed and told him I was to be a cellist. I'd told him I was going to be brilliant. I had said it just like that, just as embarrassingly, and my whole body, like my desire, had felt exposed, waiting for him to say something. But he hadn't said anything. I was stark and young and dogged.

Walking to the station, I asked if it was true that he remembered, knowing some anticipation would be evident in my voice—I couldn't hide it.

'Yeah,' he said. 'You told me all about yourself.'

We were walking under dark plane trees. He was looking at me with a small, inscrutable smile that could have been from pleasure or awkwardness, and I found this smile, I found him, riveting.

'And did you like it?'

'I liked it a lot.' He stretched his hands out, which looked strong, and I recalled being told he was a sculptor. 'Did you mean the music, just then?'

I nodded.

'I don't know if this makes sense, but it was almost too well formed.'

'Too well formed,' I repeated.

The three words rang in my mind with a clean, bell-like quality. I wanted to ask more about these words, why he'd come that evening (my fantasy was he'd come for me), but we were already under the lit awning of the station where the others were laughing over something unimportant. He checked where I was heading, and when I told him Kentish Town, he seemed disappointed. He was going in the opposite direction, he said, and so we were separated.

At home, I looked him up online. I'd done this before, so I knew there wasn't much information. At that point he wasn't successful. But there was a photograph of one of his sculptures, which was ungainly looking, tiny. I decided there must be something so particular in him, to create a thing like that, in miniature. All I can describe it as was a piece of motion.

Once our relationship was over, I spent ages looking for that photo. He'd made so much work by that point that the small, early sculpture seemed to have been lost among the rest, but after a few days I found it, and it was like looking back in time to something nascent. Fragile, tremulous.

I suppose the recital he came to was one start of things between us, and it's where I go when I start thinking of him now, yet I could still plant a flag on other places—the dark bedroom at that party, or the few times I saw him around in the years afterwards, in pubs, or at someone's birthday—and call any of those a beginning.

I'd heard through friends he was talented and had grown curious to know what, exactly, that meant. When I saw him out in places, I hoped they might be the start of something, but then we wouldn't speak—he would keep to himself, I would leave early—and a long time would pass without seeing him again, until I knew it was not to be. But, really, all of those could be the beginning because I was so aware of him, and now I know, he was also observing me, and each time I had a greater impression of him, and it was these impressions that led to that evening at the music hall, our conversation during the walk to the station with the bright trains and the dark plane trees, which felt so intimate without obviously, demonstrably, being so.

When I play my cello, when I do so in private wearing strange assortments of clothing I invariably have to take off as my work builds and I begin sweating, there comes a moment my hands, my skin, smell of the maple of its body, and the maple of its body smells of the sweat I have left there, so our two bodies seem the same, and it's as if there can be no misunderstanding between them. If someone were to see me in this state, they would see me and the instrument. They would observe a gap between us, and I would not be able to show them different until I started playing, when they would in fact hear our sameness. But I would not be able to play, to demonstrate this intimacy, if it wasn't something already established privately, just between us.

I was not surprised when I received a text from him a few days after he showed up at the recital, although the thing itself, meaning his presence in my room where he had never been, was shocking.

At that time, I was playing in this quartet, and we were preparing for a performance of Bartok's No 3. I was about to turn thirty, and for a year I had also wanted to leave the quartet, so I could focus on my career as a soloist, and because I did not like the way in which the lead violinist, who believed himself, still, the most famous of us, imposed his will on our interpretations. I often did not agree with him, or I wanted to play the music of different composers—ones we hadn't played before. That summer I had many solo performances taking place, with more in the coming autumn, including the first performances of new work by an avant-garde composer I'd met years before, and with whom I'd been collaborating.

I had not told many people my desire to be a soloist because I was not sure about my allowance of things: if it was even feasible. There was a shame in wanting things too openly—I'd learnt this through watching others enact their desires—so I worked in silence. I woke at six, back aching, to play for a few hours before I left for rehearsals each morning. It was at that hour I noticed the year turning, every day the sun a little stronger.

I rented the front room of my flat, which was on a main road, and just in front of the flat was a bus stop. The top decks of the buses were level with my windows, so when I played, if I left the curtains open, every so often I would have an audience. I would sit there for two or three hours each morning, only occasionally looking up to see a face. And then I returned home late in the evenings to find the flat deserted. My flatmate was researching her PhD on various forms of countercultural nightlife, which meant her days were reversed, and she was out until the early morning.

The quartet was to perform Bartok's No. 3, his shortest. It's a single movement, the opening part of which consists of fragments of song that build and dispel in a way that feels probing, contemplative. The music itself feels like the process of composition, in this way, so it's like you can hear Bartok's uncertainty, his hesitations. Questions over how to perform that—how to turn a process of doing and undoing into one moment, one interpretation—consumed me at the time, as it did the rest of the quartet.

The text I received from Billy said he hoped I didn't mind that he'd asked the pianist for my number. He wanted to know if I'd like to do something with him the week after, or, if not, perhaps another time. When I replied to him, saying I did want to see him that week, it was after composing and deleting and re-writing various versions of the same text. I wanted to convey keenness without making it seem desperate, or worse, untruthful, and I wanted to do this without leaving too much time, in which he might grow nervous about me responding. He sent me another text within five minutes of my reply:

Would you come to this exhibition?

There was a bright, edginess to the day that matched how I was feeling. It was May, the start of a heat wave, and the gallery was by the Thames. He was already waiting in the entrance hall when I arrived, which was a huge, overwhelming space with the proportions of an air hangar. He wore the same t-shirt and blue jeans as when I'd last seen him, and although he was tall compared to everyone else, he was also leaning against a glass wall in a way that appeared boyish. He stood up as I came towards him and we laughed, nervously, about how much we were sweating.

The exhibition entailed lots of narrow rooms made of plyboard, and each room had something inside—for example one room had a camera and the next room had a screen showing what was being recorded on it, gimmicky things like that—and the rooms were maze-like, so he said we should stick together, which we did. The pleasure of this was increased by the fact I didn't have any feelings for the art. I was glad to be free to watch him, but I was probably watching myself, too, how I moved, and whether or not I seemed attractive. In a window on the way there I'd looked different than I'd expected: messier, my skin flushed.

At first, we spoke a little about where we were living, and he confessed he'd moved back to his mum's because he could pay a cheaper rent, which left him with enough money for a studio, but soon enough he only seemed capable of looking at the exhibition. It was obvious we were both nervous to be there together, yet he seemed to grow more anxious with every room. I'd assumed he wanted to take me there so he could enjoy being the authority—he obviously knew a lot more about contemporary art than me—except it was difficult for him to take that role when the art was terrible.

He kept saying things like, *there's probably more to it* or, *we're probably missing something*. I nodded without saying much, and this seemed to make things worse, and the way this came out was that he would locate exactly what was wrong with the art, what was unoriginal, but attempt to make a case for why it wasn't. The more I went along with this, the tenser he became, as if he knew what I was doing, but he couldn't bring himself to say so.

When we made it to the last room there was a spotlight in the ceiling that went on and off and when it came on there was a wall of pornographic photos. He just said,

'Ah.'

Because there was nothing else to say. Standing there with the light flashing I did start to laugh, and then it was like something in him finally gave way, and he said, yes, it was awful.

Maybe because we wanted to rectify this, we ended up at mine afterwards, where we fucked immediately. We came together greedily, and he became less shy then. My room was full of the noise of cars and mopeds through the open windows. He lifted me and pulled my hair, and I felt the strength of his body. His sculptures had grown larger, he told me, as if it was their own decision. He was finding them physically exhausting to make.

He left before midnight. As he dressed, quietly in the dark, he apologised for the exhibition and asked if I'd had a good time anyway. I told him not to say that. I had, and I realised how much I had, how much I wanted him to stay, even though I had to be up early for rehearsals. It was impossible, anyway, because I needed sleep, which I explained, and he did seem understanding of this, in the beginning. When he got down to the street he turned and waved at me where I was leaning, smiling, out the window.

There was an exhibition of his sculptures shown here, in London, recently. I saw the posters on tube platforms with his name written sideways in thin, red letters. It was a beautiful red, full of blue, without much yellow. I decided he must've chosen that. He must have wanted to have his name hung sideways, so it wasn't immediately legible.

It is always startling to see his name in public. I find it too real. I suppose this is because his name usually feels illusory; I don't speak to anyone who knows him anymore, and I can't remember the last time I said his name out loud. So, his continued existence feels in many ways a fantasy, one I can deny most of the time, until I'm confronted by it. Just like how those brightly lit tube platforms seem less real once I'm back up on the surface, underneath the sky, moving about the city.

Sometimes I think about all the people who enjoy his work and go often to see it, and how they must feel their own private things for his sculptures, and perhaps they think they know him when they see his name. Perhaps they do know him. But, for me, in that moment, he felt invisible. And I believe I have known how that feels myself, to feel invisible in the moments I am most seen, and so has he, and finding his name like that reminded me of this. It was too intimate, really.

The second time we saw each other, he came over to mine again late in the evening, after I'd finished practice, and I showed him my instrument. He seemed more assured than I'd expected in handling its body. He placed his forefinger at the base of the neck and traced the curve of the upper bout, crouching in front of it, looking at the grain of the maple as his finger travelled to its waist.

The cello I played then is the same I still play. I was gifted it whilst I was studying, and it is a rare cello, one I was first loaned a long time before, for a prestigious competition where I came second. I'd played on several valuable cellos before that point, ones that had been loaned to me for other competitions, and also, I'd played on many rented instruments as my body changed and developed. The bodies of my cello were transient, they grew too. I was never with one cello until this one.

My current cello was made in the eighteenth century, by an Italian luthier whose instruments, including other cellos and many violins, are believed to be superior to others. A lot of people believe this and many contest it, and there have been experiments and investigations into the sound quality of various instruments, none of which have been conclusive. There is a theory, which says these instruments, made during this time period, are better because they are made from the denser wood of trees grown when the world's temperature dropped. There were not as many sunspots, apparently, so all the trees grew slower in the cold and were stunted. I do not much care because it is my cello, and I need it.

At first, I enjoyed watching Billy stroke its body, although I did not take my eyes from his finger. But then I did mind. He lingered too long, so I removed his hand.

'I know how to be careful with things,' he said. 'I'm careful with things all the time.'

I could not explain myself because care was not the problem. I was not concerned with damage. It was my cello. Although many other cellists had played it before, I felt it was mine, and perhaps it was because of that tenuous ownership that I was so possessive. And also, I didn't know if he *was* careful.

The unease of the moment must have passed because I told him about the sunspots, about the cold, dense, wood of centuries before. I told him also about Mstislav Rostropovich lying his cello on its side, as a boy, squeezing his small bum into the c bout—the curved dip in its middle, where Billy's finger had rested. I touched the spot, saying he would stick his bum right in and remain like that, because it was what he needed to play the thing, he could not help himself. An old professor had told me this as a way of demonstrating it was no dignified passion that I was involved in.

According to my parents, I was five when I first told them I wanted to play the cello. Neither they nor I can remember where I got the idea of this instrument. It was, they say, as if the idea seized me, and I couldn't untangle myself. Perhaps I'd seen someone play, or heard it, or perhaps I'd only noticed its round, gleaming body hanging in the window of a music shop like a bright, fresh, carcass.

When I next saw my mother, I mentioned Billy. It was the first time I'd had anyone to tell her about. She often asked after my romantic life, but I'd never known what to say—to me, my romantic life was obvious, it played out on the stage. This thing with Billy was different. We were in the kitchen of my parents' house, and my dad was in the garden, hanging up washing. She was talking about something else, and I shocked myself by becoming impatient to tell her everything. Billy was having this effect on me.

'I'm surprised you've had time to contemplate someone,' she said, when I did tell her. 'You're usually so strict with yourself.'

My mother, after the first time she'd seen me on stage, tried to talk me out of performing. She claimed that beneath the spotlights I cast no shadow, and the transience of this state disturbed her.

I told my dad about Billy too, over dinner, and he kept shushing my mother as she tried to talk about other things although I did not have much more to say—I couldn't tell them how Billy and I had just been meeting late at night, even if only to spend an hour in bed together before he left again. There was an avarice in this that I found thrilling because it felt equal. A joint desire to absorb the physicality of the other, to come in this way to communion. But I didn't have anything certain to relate, except that he was a sculptor.

At this my mother showed some interest. She asked me to explain what form his sculptures took. When I said I didn't know, I hadn't yet seen them, she took her long hair down and sighed. Her work was in metaphysics, she was a professor—form was something interesting to her. She wanted to know why I hadn't tried to gain more information.

'This will tell you a lot,' she said. 'Ask him how the shape of things come to him—how things gain clarity.'

'He'll understand,' my dad interjected. 'About your practice.'

My mother raised her chin a fraction.

'Do you think so?'

'But he does already,' I said, rushing the words, feeling strongly that I wanted to prove something I did not yet feel sure of. 'He understands perfectly.'

The first piece of clarity he offered was whilst I was in Florence for a performance with the quartet. The warm air was fragrant, not yet oppressive, and, in reply to a text I'd sent about wanting to see him, he wrote:

Being with you is what I want in general

(I hope you know)

I grew lightheaded about this. I told him the same.

That night I leant out of my hotel window listening to young people sing as they strolled up and down the busy road below. Their voices were like chants, it seemed, on the breeze, up to the rooftops.

He'd spoken to me about the Boboli gardens in that city, so I went a day later. I took photos of the sculptures that were there, to send him, because he'd never been, and now all I can remember of those gardens is pacing about looking at my phone, either taking photos or checking if he'd replied yet. After those initial texts, we'd continued talking about an album that had just been released by a singer from America, whose songs were sparse and sensual. I'd sent a text that was disparaging about this woman, and I worried about this after because I'd called her shallow and selfish, which was uncompromising, although I did think the songs were selfish, her voice was too breathy. I didn't understand what she was saying.

I worried I'd ruined the sentiments of our earlier messages by revealing a more judgemental side of myself. In the time before he replied, I paced around correcting the bad message in my head, fearing he might not respond. I wondered how terrible this might feel, if I could save things by sending another text. Then the gardens seemed dark and the plants too abundant, the people quick, pushy. But soon he did reply. He agreed about the singer. Once he had replied, of course it seemed obvious that he would've, but, in these moments, it always felt like I was leaping without knowing if I might land safely, if something might get broken.

Reading his reply, it was like his body was there beside me. Coming upon the pale figures of statuary among the foliage, I sent him more photos of the gardens. What I did not have photos of was the narrow, steep venue where we'd performed, every row occupied by people fanning themselves with programmes. The heat outside the venue had reached inside, and the smell was musky, like the streets, like the churches. The vista of heads had moved as one body when we crossed the stage, straightening and twisting. I wished I could've shown him that.

Immediately after, I had a performance of Louise Farrenc's sonatas in Edinburgh as part of a programme of female composers, which got some attention. And then another with the quartet in Oxford, where it was so hot a woman in the audience fainted. The violinist did not like to stop unless it was a heart attack, so we played on whilst three stewards jostled the woman out, her long yellow skirt wrapping and unwrapping about her ankles.

I hadn't been able to see Billy during all those days of performance, but he'd started sending me photos of the light in his studio each morning. He arrived about the same time I woke, so he could work for a few hours before starting his shift at the removals company he was employed by. I would make sure that these images were some of the first things I saw, as I washed my face or ate breakfast, although I did not reply until later. At that time, I did not know I could tell him about this thing with the photos, how a piece of his perspective was the first thing I wanted to see every day. I suppose this is because I'd never had an impulse like that before, with someone, and I did not realise I could reveal it so simply. My feelings felt too unpractised. I did not yet know how to present them.

The images showed only the ceiling of the studio, which was pitched, with a skylight. The fact of the floor, of his work, was kept out of view, and my curiosity grew with every photo. It was the end of the season, a time of year I usually felt depleted, and yet this thing with him was leaving me full of energy.

When I did see him in his studio, for the first time, I paused before crossing the threshold. The room was in a disused office building, and the floor was littered with containers of plaster, various buckets of dried material, and old pieces of paper, whilst around the room were the sculptures, none of which appeared finished. There were also many smaller versions of the larger works made of clay, which he explained were studies, and I liked these. *Casts*, he called them. They were all over the place. It was a crowded room, which I'd not been prepared for. I had the feeling of being at the heart of a storm—all around me was movement.

When he first started taking me about, he was awkward; he showed me a few of the casts and the sculptures, but every time he tried to explain what they meant, he became dissatisfied with his explanations.

'I'm not making sense,' he kept saying.

He would trail off mid-sentence as we were talking to look at one of them and an emotion—pleasure or its opposite—would pass, nakedly, over his features. I'm not sure if it was because of the sculptures themselves, or the seriousness with which he treated them, but there was the uncanny sense, somehow, that they were sentient, these things. He asked if I liked them, and I did. I was in many ways bewildered by them. Do you really, he asked again.

'Yes,' I laughed, 'yes.'

'Well, I'm vain.' He was wearing a dark cotton shirt and trousers, both stiff with plaster. 'I haven't shown anything in ages.'

'Are you worried?'

'My mum thinks I should keep going. But she likes me living there.'

'And your dad?'

I couldn't remember him mentioning his father.

'He doesn't exactly care.'

He picked up a small clay model and walked over to a corner where he placed it on a stool, in the shadows, moving it into different positions until he seemed satisfied. Then he came back beside me, into the sunlight.

I really hadn't seen anything like those sculptures before. They looked like unidentified organisms, and just like the earlier sculpture I'd seen on the internet, they seemed full of the possibility of motion even though they were stationary, so I had the impression they were things that had been caught in the process of growth, or perhaps, of disintegration. This process, or the idea of process, seemed to be their subject. It was only from certain angles, when I wasn't looking straight at them, that I also had the impression they were pieces of machinery—quite the opposite to how they seemed when I looked at them directly.

He always worked with plaster, and he started showing me the ways in which the large pieces had to be supported by metal rods, growing more animated as he did so. He demonstrated how he might begin making something, and his voice became fuller. It was as if it broke open. Everything was about craft, he explained, it was always about the craft of them, about the differing nature of the plaster, the ease with which they would break. He spoke about their rigidity, and I enjoyed the sense of that. I considered if rigid was something he was, too, just as I was. It did seem like a quality we might find in each other.

Listening to him, I began to find the situation unbearably erotic. I knew, instinctively, we would not have sex, that he would not see me sexually in that room, could not, there was not enough space for it. I don't know why I wanted him to see me sexually there. Perhaps I only wanted my body to take precedence over these others—

all these forms he gave his attention. But I felt, also, that I could see him better among them, that I could see new parts of him, which were commanding. He touched them, and I wanted him to touch me, as I remembered him doing, and in this, I both did and did not feel like one of them.

He used to write out lists detailing the characteristics of his pieces, and these included things like what they would smell like, how they might move, if they could speak, what tone of voice they would use, what they might say, what they would want to communicate. It was about becoming intimate with them, he explained, when I discovered these lists, which were the ragged sheets of paper coating the floor of his studio.

After seeing his posters on the tube recently, I recalled these lists. I tried to make one of his characteristics. I wrote down his smell, its slightly chalky quality, the exact softness of his voice, the tonal registers it moved through, when it moved through them, why it would. Quickly, the list became full of things, but then reading it back I was dissatisfied. For each word, I wanted to add another, and I didn't want to add this word beside it but on top, or below, so the words might be layered. Often what I wanted to add was an antonym. I had written attentive, for example, but then I also wanted to write aloof. And I didn't mean that at times his behaviour differed, but that he was both of these things at once. Somehow it was only when the words were together that I saw him.

Something I used to love was watching him sketch and watching him do this was about observing an instance of manifestation, without really being able to locate it. For a long time, there would be nothing but lines on the page, then shapes, movement. Abruptly, at some point, these things would lead to the emergence of an image: a face, an object—a pattern. After this, I would ask him to take me back: at what point did it emerge? What stroke of his hand had created, from lines, familiarity? There must've been one moment that did it, and this was the moment I wanted—nothing, something. The point at which you recognise what is facing you.

I was envious of his ability in this. I was envious, too, of the image. The product of his hand. It contained resolve just by appearing. It seemed in many ways to will itself, and I wanted to know how something might do that. How it came to be indisputable.

By July, the heat of that summer remained unbroken. The sky was a perfect, resolute blue, and often I saw pink, swollen feet sticking out of open windows. I worked with the composer throughout this time. At that point, he was in his early forties, well established after achieving some success with a series of neo-classical pieces for violin and piano, which utilised electronics, long periods of silence, and were sometimes described as challenging. He was now interested in a purer examination of emotion, one that might portray the gap between belief and experience.

We had met in Venice, four years earlier, at the bar after a performance I'd given of Janáček's *Pohádka*, which musically re-tells the story of an epic Russian poem, but only does so in glimpses. This was whilst I was still living in Paris, where I'd studied at a conservatoire under a female cellist whose name had overshadowed mine for a long time after. The composer had approached me to begin speaking about Luigi Nono, the equality of silence and sound in his music. He'd told me he'd seen my performance.

'Do you know your cello is the voice I've been searching for?' he said. 'I yelped when you started.'

I'd heard that yelp. I'd assumed he was very drunk, which he was, but we'd started emailing, and I'd been amazed to find his sentiments unchanged. He wanted to work with me. During my final months in Paris, before I returned to London, we spoke regularly. He had trouble with the industry because he regarded himself as an outsider, and he was not commercially minded, even though he'd had some success, which meant little in the way of promotion for his work. When he did get offered interviews, he was often required to speak mainly about the industry itself, which he did not want to spend more time on. He wanted to speak about his music. He told me to be careful about things, because the industry only liked replicas. I felt I had things easier than him, yet things were not always easy.

It was to him I'd confessed my fears over an inability to be loving, when it seemed I could not find someone who would fit into the narrow leeway of my ambition, when I felt nothing for any of the men I met. In response to this, he told me not to worry because I played my cello like I was fucking it. After that I began to notice how my body moved, how it performed, how the instrument indented my thighs as my legs spread around it. I looked up definitions of the word *erotic* and found it came in many guises, like focus, or dedication, and it was not always beautiful, or romantic, to make something.

That summer we were involved in our final preparations before we started performing some of the composer's new work in the autumn, and I spent as much time as I could at his basement flat with his collection of tortoiseshell rabbits. I was speaking to the composer, and I was speaking to Billy, and sometimes I was surprised to find my voice on the phone change depending on who was on the other end. Perhaps I was less forceful with Billy. Perhaps I was more serious with the composer. I was confused, because I did not feel different around Billy, but perhaps I felt, simply, less certain. With the composer I always felt certain, even when we, together, were uncertain on something, I always knew what I was doing, but I hadn't expected Billy. I did not always know how to go about having him.

Love, as an idea, was not yet much on my mind, seeming too abstract for the greedy actions of our bodies, but there was a growing concentration to my experience, a peeling off of the edges. I had an awareness of it when I told the composer about Billy.

'But you're not serious!' he replied.

Perhaps because he understood I was conveying this change in my perceptions. I'd told him about Billy because we'd been studying my schedule, trying to fit in more rehearsals before autumn. I had a performance of Elgar coming up, with a famous orchestra, for which I'd been preparing all year, and it was this, the idea that I'd entered into a relationship whilst I had so much critical work to do, which made him ask the question. I knew why he had. The Elgar was the largest opportunity I'd been offered. I knew it seemed an odd choice to start a relationship just then, for I had never before done it, and the composer's question, really, was about imbalance, whether it suggested a change in me that might affect the work we did together.

His consideration: if I was telling him about Billy then the thing between us meant something, and if it meant something, was there a danger it might come to mean everything?

This was becoming my own. My past was littered with nights in stranger's beds, but they stood alone; I'd never allowed them to accumulate. These were men whose faces I could no longer recall, whose smells had grown sour by morning. Many had been musicians that I'd met at competitions or festivals, who I'd gone on to beat in the eyes of the judges or the critics, or who'd beaten me. But they did not matter. Their lips and fingers were at the boundaries, beyond the spotlights. The performance had been the thing. And now something did matter, and I detected, too, a note of possessiveness in the composer's question, which I did not begrudge him—I, after all, was his instrument. He did not want things in between us.

Late at night, I revealed my nerves about the Elgar to Billy. We were lying entangled in my bed, our heads on the same pillow, and I was preoccupied with my interpretation. He asked what I was thinking, so I told him, probably at length, of the difficulties I was having without stopping to provide any context. I was so absorbed by this piece of music, and had been since I was young, that I could not conceive of it needing context. I spoke about the issue of doing something novel, the line it was important to tread between what felt new and what felt truthful. I spoke about Beatrice Harrison and Jacqueline du Pré.

He stopped me. 'Are they cellists?'

'Oh,' I replied. 'Yes.'

I did not continue speaking. From the way I did not do this, my shock must have been evident. After a few moments he said, if he was honest, he didn't listen to it—*classical music*. He'd heard of Elgar, but he wouldn't recognise his pieces. He had no clue what a concerto was, as opposed to other things I'd mentioned: sonatas, suites.

'I don't actually know the names of any cellists.' He looked down at our knees. 'I want to know,' he said. 'I want to be able to talk with you about it.'

I felt foolish, and beyond that I sensed something more alarming: a certain narrowness to my mind that could suggest snobbishness. I wanted to explain that it did not matter to me that he did not know about Elgar.

I knew Elgar did not matter in the broader sense, in the sense of the universal. In fact, Elgar probably mattered too much in this sense, had been given far too much importance, but this did not change the fact that for a cellist, Elgar was paramount.

I tried to clarify this, and we met, once more, in confusion.

'I know,' he said, and he seemed further hurt. 'I want to know about Elgar because you *are* a cellist.'

Something, some twitch in my brain that I could never anticipate, led me to say,

'Oh, not really.'

And I was puzzled into silence.

Why diminish myself—I was a cellist. Even if at times I felt I was not good enough to claim the title, I still played the cello, it was my profession, why was I uneasy, in certain moments, of allowing this?

I got up. On my laptop, I found the recording of Jacqueline du Pré performing the Elgar in the sixties, with her husband, Daniel Barenboim, conducting, and I played it for Billy. A concerto is just a piece of music for an entire orchestra, I told him, with a solo part, which is sometimes, although rarely, a cello. He asked why it was rare, so I said, for a long time, many composers did not have faith in the cello.

'They didn't think it could hold its own against an orchestra,' I said. 'They didn't understand it.'

As we watched du Pré perform, I realised how long it had been since I'd done so. It was something I had done religiously, as a child, before I had understood my own expression, when all I'd wanted was the force of hers. I explained the spiccato of the second movement to Billy, when the bow had to bounce, why it was technical. How she built to such a precise, searching forte by playing her bow slowly, near the bridge—how she knew to hold something of herself back, to allow the music its own emotion. I knew the recording by heart—when she throws her long hair back, how the creases of her silk dress are exposed under the spotlights. Her body, decorated by such femininity, is not often elegant, nor modest. She does not perform in any manner that could be expected. She is violent, I think. It's a controlled violence. She shifts between notes almost too quickly for the recording to make sense of, except that the music emanates from these movements. In this way, there is endless sense to what she is doing. It is as if the music is just then being written.

It was hard to interpret the look on Billy's face, although he seemed rapt by whatever he was feeling. We were sitting beside each other on the edge of the bed, the laptop balanced on his bare knees. I told him, her performance was so singular because it was always surprising, and yet at the same time it sounded settled, like hearing a truth that's undeniable, as if nothing could have been different.

'And this is music that's been played thousands of times with as many interpretations,' I said.

It almost made me sick to consider. Because how do you get to that point, I asked him, how do you ever become so certain.

The lead violinist of the orchestra I was to perform the Elgar with sprained his wrist tenderising a piece of chicken. It was not believed to be serious, and I was assured he would recover in time, but it introduced a mood of uncertainty to the approaching concert, which seemed to spread. The quartet had its first rehearsal for the upcoming season where an argument broke out between the two violinists over an errant bow stroke. The men fought viciously with each other, whilst the violist and I sat in silence, holding our instruments in futility. Shortly after, the composer grew unsure about various sections of the piece he had written, and the afternoons I spent with him became arduous. He obsessed over minute decisions, then, when we were not together, he would send endless emails, requesting I record myself playing variations of the same passages.

I was starting to become confused in my interpretations. Often, I was spending all night practising, trying different fingerings and adjusting my hold, plates of partially eaten toast accumulating around me as I attempted to be better, always, to gain control.

On a free evening, I took the train to Billy's studio. It had been a humid, airless day, and he'd opened the skylight so that a breeze might enter, which occasionally stirred the carpet of paper. We hadn't been able to see each other for five days, and I spent a while explaining about the demands of everyone I was working with, my own demands of myself. I was full of desire at this time, and it astonishes me to remember that—my capacity for torment.

Billy expressed surprise about the agency I had in the composer's music.

'But I know more about the cello than he does,' I replied. 'It's my instrument.'

I was sitting in the centre of the room, on the floor, where he'd begun sketching me. It was still so hot I'd taken my clothes off. I hadn't done this before, sat for him like that. He came over to straighten or bend my limbs into the angles he wanted, lingering over them for a moment before retreating to the wall. He seemed to make quick work of each sketch before turning the page and starting another.

'Do you get scared of the audience?' he said, after a while. 'If you look.'

'When the lights are up?'

'When you're playing.'

'Not *scared*.' His eyes were on my wrist, which was resting on my stomach. 'Sometimes, after, I wonder what they see.'

'What do you think?'

'I try not to think of anything.'

He smiled. The sunlight had begun to shift from my body.

'I'd feel like nothing, too,' he said, putting his pad of paper down, 'I couldn't do it.'

The night seemed too hot to sleep. Neither of us wanted it to be over, so we stayed in his studio late, drinking tequila, passing limes between us, a half-moon edging into the frame of the skylight. By the time we made it back to my flat, we were tipsy. We lay on the bed for some time looking at that same moon, and I asked if he wanted to hear it, the Elgar. When he said he did, the speed with which he replied made it seem like something he'd already thought about. I'd given him one of my tickets to the concert, which was meant to be the first time he'd watch me perform, but then it seemed obvious he should see me alone, not on the stage.

'Do you really?' I said, and he nodded. So, that was how I first played for him.

The windows onto the street were wide open, and he lay on the bed with one arm and one leg thrown out sideways. I played for him in fragments, sometimes repeating a section if he asked, sometimes going back to the beginning and starting again, if I wanted. We hadn't turned any of the lights on, for some reason. One side of his body was illuminated by the streetlights and the same light must have illuminated me from his vantage point. He fell asleep in the end, and I kept playing as the night quietened.

I don't always think of him lying there when I hear the Elgar, when I play it, but sometimes I do. I remember the half-moon, the smell of the limes, the warm night. I have the sense of it being somewhere else entirely, where we went together.

Although there have been opportunities in the years since we ended, I've always been wary of seeing his sculptures. I haven't been able to avoid them completely, but mostly I've been afraid to know what they might reveal—some trouble or some bliss, something visible beneath their surfaces that might betray the grain of his experience, how it is. Recently, though, I visited his exhibition. I believe I wanted, after all, to feel that grain again. Or maybe I just let thoughts of it in, and the thing took on a largeness, a curiosity that the posters on the tube could not satisfy.

It was, in many ways, like coming back to parts of his body and doing so among a crowd and feeling I should not be there. These things used to frighten me; these things—his sculptures—used to fill me with love and with dread.

The pieces were new, so I did not recognise them, but their presence in the gallery, how restless they felt, was familiar. Their texture, the sense of his hands, was familiar. I couldn't decide how to approach them, and I moved around each one holding my breath, anticipating they might smell of him, but they didn't, they were neutral, distant. There were blocks of writing on the walls detailing the work, including notes he'd written, and I read these a few times without learning anything. I had to crane my neck over other heads to read about Andalusia, where we once lived, but it was written about in ways that made it feel like nowhere I'd visited. There was a photo of the house we'd lived in, except the proportions of the home seemed altered. Not at all how I remembered.

Throughout the exhibition he was referred to as the artist, and my name, obviously, was never mentioned. But my presence was alluded to in some sections. It was alluded to in ways that only I would detect. I wanted to say something, after viewing these things, and yet I did not know what I wanted to say. I did not know if it was possible for me to say anything. These objects were his. I do not have such objects.

There was a long, celebratory piece written about the exhibition for a newspaper, which featured halfway down, a large, beautiful, photograph of him. When I read the article, I was shocked to find I that I had taken this photo. I had forgotten it. Sunlight glances the side of his face, on his cheekbone, and in many ways he seems perfect. I confess that I have stared at this image many times since it was published. An image of my own eye, but within it I feel none of my own agency. I look at it, into a past that has been taken, and I think—how was it taken?

He phoned, a few days after that evening together, to say he'd been working on some models from the sketches. It was strange, he said, because he'd been working on my body, so it felt like we'd been together, and then he realised he wasn't going to see me. The idea of the models was peculiar. Something I hadn't, at all, expected. I remembered what he'd asked me that night, and I tried to imagine how he might see me—if the models would feel familiar, if I would recognise them.

His voice was soft, as if he'd just woken. I wanted to go to him. I was right at the end of my practice, in the middle of replacing my C string, which had snapped, leaving a cut on my forearm. I had to be at the composer's early in the morning, before I went to rehearse with the quartet, so I needed sleep. I couldn't go to him. He said he already knew that, but didn't I have to live outside of my instrument?

'I have been.'

'It's tiring.'

'Well,' I said, because I couldn't think of what else to say. It was tiring. 'You haven't told me what you want with this.'

'I just did. You said no, so what do you want?'

'You, obviously, but you can't have every minute.'

When we hung up it was strangely formal, and I stood there licking the blood off my arm wondering if that might be it. The fragility seemed shocking. The sudden formality, the wrenching away of my expectations. I knew in one way I had gone against my interests, and the urge to call him back was a difficult one to overcome. I did not want him to end things, which now felt possible. There was an understanding and I'd been disruptive. I had not done what we both wanted.

I finished replacing the string and continued my practice, but I had an unnerving sense of diffusion, as if I was in more than a single place at once. I felt the body I inhabited was no longer my only body—there was also the object in his mind, which his hands, just then, were bringing into being. And I could no longer say which of these was the true form. I was no longer the authority.

I said love was not much on my mind, and as a construct it wasn't. I had no sense of falling. He was not the only thing that existed for me. This does not mean there was no extremity of feeling. I understood it through as a sense of surrender: it was the laying aside of other ways of being. Now, not seeing him did not just mean thwarting his desire, but thwarting my own, which was the extremity—I needed him. This need was the sharp edge I slid along.

We were supposed to have dinner with my friends the night after that conversation. My rehearsals during the day went poorly because I hadn't heard from him in the morning, nothing to make amends. I sent him a text at lunchtime asking if he still wanted to come to the dinner, and he didn't reply for ages, so I had an overwhelming sense of failure. Then he did reply, saying obviously he was still coming, he was looking forward to it, and would I send him the address of my friends' flat so he could meet me there.

The couple we were having dinner with were two older women I'd met whilst studying in Paris. One was a harpist and the other an oboist, though they both played a variety of things, and, in fact, the harpist had helped me overcome a fundamental weakness in my fourth finger at the start of my career. They'd lived together for years in a thin, ornate flat, which was cramped by instruments. It smelt of old sheet music and bow rosin, and I worried about Billy being in that space, which was so much more mine than his. But he was already there when I arrived. He was drinking wine with my friends at the dinner table, wearing a white shirt. My friends were in dark clothes of many layers, and the walls were entirely covered by bookshelves, whilst on the floor behind his chair was a trumpet, its gold corresponding to the pale gold of his hair, as if it had been placed there deliberately. They seemed to be asking him a lot of questions about his sculptures, and I could tell immediately they were taking his shyness for modesty, which in some ways it was.

I hadn't expected him to arrive first, so I was caught off guard. I fumbled around in the kitchen with the wine I'd brought, and when the oboist took it from me, I asked for a glass immediately and waited by the counter, restlessly, as she poured it.

At the table, she began asking, pointedly, about the Elgar, how I was coping, and then the harpist wanted to know if Billy had seen the recording of Jacqueline du Pré's performance. He said yes, I'd shown him, and he'd watched it more than once because he was interested by the movements of her body.

'What exactly are you interested in?' the harpist said, pushing her glasses up off her face.

Except he couldn't say. He looked at me a little helplessly, so I started talking about du Pré's relationship with Daniel Barenboim, how intense it was, and how important it was to see her performance as one that was also for her lover, which both played into, and played against, expectations of her femininity. He nodded, he said that was what he meant, and I was more relaxed afterwards.

My friends left us briefly at the table to finish preparing dinner, and Billy turned to me. He looked pristine in that crowded room. I started to tell him how useless my practice had been, how he was right, I should've come to see him, but he interrupted me, apologising. He'd come up with something, he said, something that felt real. He was planning to start a bigger sculpture from the sketches he'd made of me.

'If that's ok—I couldn't stop thinking about it.'

'Of course, that's ok. I thought you were angry.'

'No, really?' He put his hand on my shoulder. 'I was just busy, sorry. I wasn't angry.'

I wondered if it was the idea, or telling me, or being there, which had caused him to look so excited. The harpist came back to light the candles on the table, and the flames rose before us, and their light spread up the bookshelves. The room was cluttered with objects—concert posters, heavy, chrome lamps, a Steinway upright—that my friends had accumulated over their life together, and they lent the moment a sense of constancy. I wasn't sure how to understand this idea of his, but I did know it was something he was willing to dedicate himself to, and I was its substance.

Perhaps because of this, or because of the wine, I started to feel better. I spoke with my friends about the industry, a conductor recently accused of assault, whilst we ate the lasagne they'd cooked, and afterwards they told Billy the story of their careers. They spoke at the same time, correcting each other over details of this story, but it was the same as I'd always heard it—their emergence onto the New York stage in the nineties, their return to Europe in the sombre years after 9/11—the moments of success and failure. I wondered how it felt for them to be sat together, after so long, in that room full of objects. Billy was quiet, but he was also attentive, and I was more pleased than I'd expected to have someone on my side of the table.

Just before midnight the harpist produced some grappa, and whilst she poured it into our glasses, she returned to Jacqueline du Pré.

'He was enthralled to her,' she said about Barenboim. 'Billy, that's what I wanted to say about that performance—it's so rarely the case a man can show that.'

'And are they still together?' he said.

We all turned to him.

'She's long dead,' the oboist replied. 'You didn't look her up?'

The base of his cheeks turned brilliantly red, and I squeezed his thigh, gently, beneath the table.

'She was young,' I told him. 'It doesn't matter. It's just what most people know about her.'

'Well, the illness was a shock. She was relentlessly the star,' the harpist said.

'Yes, enthralled or not,' the oboist cut in, emptying her glass, 'she died, and he kept going, and that's it.'

The Elgar has become known as a painful piece of music, and Billy always seemed to find it so. Throughout our relationship, if I put it on, he would become remote, troubled. I believe the music affected him, and a lot of that could've been down to the two ways he saw me perform it: first that night, when we were in my bedroom, and I allowed him to see me as I was, with my cello, and then in a large concert hall, watching me at the dead centre of the spotlights.

I worried the Elgar reminded him of the way, at that time, my artistry took precedence over everything. But I see now that's not the entire picture, because the night I played it privately for him must have been the first night we were in love together.

Sometimes, still, when I play my cello, I imagine him sitting across from me. My memories are full of us, looking at each other across rooms, or concert halls. They go on relentlessly—his eyes find mine, the notes come in and out of key, but his face stays young, focused. He watches me and I cannot think what he witnesses.

The Elgar has become known for its tragedy, yet I've never found it so painful. As a composition it is stripped back, it moves away from the romance of what Elgar had done before, to reveal something quieter about loss, about resignation. What I hear and have heard in all the bodies I've seen play it, is an expression of something more compelling. An act of endurance.

For the performance I wore a red, sleeveless dress with a high collar, which was corseted and had been my mother's. It went well, and I was cautiously pleased. Afterwards there were drinks with the event organisers, the conductor, members of the orchestra, and the composer, who'd been in the audience.

When I first found Billy backstage, at the end of the concert, he looked sickly. He didn't say much, although he did say it was good, but I was careful not to seem too pleased in case he hadn't enjoyed it. Every time anyone spoke to him during the drinks, he appeared to panic. We were all perhaps too loud and boisterous from the frenzy of nerves we'd experienced beforehand, and I was worried he felt lost, yet I didn't feel able to spend time with him because I wanted to speak with the others. It was important. It didn't ever seem enough to be capable; I had to be pleasing. I wanted the conductor to like me because he was also director of the orchestra, and I wanted to work with them again.

After a while, to my relief, Billy seemed to relax, and I saw him speaking with one of the trumpeters—I believe they were talking about another artist. When we left, everyone hugged him as well, and I felt drunk although I'd barely been drinking, delighted to the point I was becoming tempestuous. I worried I might become quarrelsome, so the composer offered to take my cello, and I suggested walking home to Billy because I didn't want to get carried away with myself.

My hands were shaking, and he asked a passer-by for a cigarette, which we shared even though I didn't smoke. It made me lightheaded, but it was comforting to do something with my hands, gratifying to pass something back and forth between us. I asked him, cautiously, whilst he smoked the cigarette, why he'd seemed so shocked after the performance.

'I did?'

He told me it was nothing, he'd been happy. But as we kept walking, we discussed the audience, and he said he'd spoken to the woman next to him before it started, who was an Elgar fanatic.

'She asked if I'd seen your performance earlier this summer, and I didn't know which one she meant.' He passed me the cigarette. 'She was telling me all about you.'

'Did you say who you were?'

'No, I didn't.'

He dodged around a group of teenagers. He told me he'd heard other people mentioning me in the audience too, and my name, repeated so much, had started to sound unfamiliar. He wasn't sure who they were discussing, who I'd be when I walked out, if I might be revealed as someone else. I was fascinated by this idea—this resistance to the performance—which I hadn't expected.

'And when I did?'

We navigated our way through a procession of cyclists.

'Well, you *were* different,' he said.

This made me laugh.

'I mean, it was grand,' he added. 'I don't know.'

He realised it was stupid, he explained, but he'd expected it to feel the same as when I'd played for him in my bedroom. It had felt instead like different music.

'It changed,' he said. 'I didn't know it would.'

After watching me play, then rising and applauding, and walking down the aisle, silent in the noisy crowd, and not remembering where to find me, he had felt lost and alone, and he regretted not telling the woman who he was. He started to believe I would ignore him. It had taken this feeling a while to fade.

None of this had been what I suspected, when I saw him looking pale, but I was not insulted, as he seemed to fear. He threw the cigarette away.

'I just didn't think I was like that,' he said. 'I thought all I'd feel was proud of you.'

A few months ago, I gave a performance at a tiny theatre in Soho, and beforehand someone asked if I was frightened. The person was another cellist, and he did so in the foyer, as groups of people broke and converged around us. I did not know how to answer. It reminded me of things I couldn't bear to remember, but also at that moment I was thinking, *yes*, except it was a feeling I didn't want to admit.

I was angry about being asked by that cellist in particular. He was someone Billy and I had dinner with, once, at a restaurant in Canary Wharf that was too expensive and filled with work parties. It was the wrong place for us. Billy was just then enjoying an initial period of success, and I'd gone through an odd, difficult event, and this had led to a change occurring between he and I, which I found humiliating: he had become my protector. This had happened suddenly, without discussion, and with this man, whom I knew better, Billy took on this role, throughout the meal intercepting questions from him on my behalf. Perhaps this was so humiliating because it was what I needed Billy to do. I needed him to intercept questions from another cellist.

I can recall Billy's arms as he did this. He would place one arm before me on the table, which was made of grey marble, and the other behind, on the top of my chair, so I was held between the space of his two arms, and this felt both secure and shocking. I wasn't eating much; the manoeuvrings of the process seemed in that bright, busy restaurant, too hard, and so the feeling I associate most with this display from Billy is hunger.

In the foyer of the theatre, I didn't want to answer this cellist's question because I knew he would link any answer to that past version of myself. That was the idea he had of me. I had seen in his eyes and heard in his tone, during the dinner, that he had not found Billy's behaviour strange, or my own, even though it was, and in the foyer, I could tell the question of fright was directed to me as a woman rather than as a musician. And I did feel scared.

What I'd understood, at the dinner, was that I needed protection, though I do not know if my need came before or after Billy's performance of it. Perhaps I only wanted security once it was something he began to offer. So, it's as if Billy taught me that fear.

There is something I return to: Billy standing bare chested in the middle of a garden, looking up to where I'm standing at an open window, his chest brown from the sun and his hair damp on his forehead. I see him raise one arm straight to the sky for my attention, and I hear what he says, but it's as if I'm far off, out in some expanse of water. The canopies of the trees behind him flatten as the wind moves over the landscape—he is calling over the air and I begin to lose the words. All I'm sure of is the breeze is moving. Still, I feel it move me.

Really, I should've asked that cellist *frightened of what?* But I suppose I did not say that because I knew, have known, the answer.

By the time it grew cold that year, Billy and I had developed a rhythm. We'd both work late into the evening, then he'd come to my flat around eleven, when my flatmate would be leaving, and we'd sit on the edge of my bed, talking each other through our days, his voice always quieter as he skimmed over events at the removals company. When he got to speaking about his own work, his voice would grow more deliberate, so I knew he wanted me to share this view of himself as an artist, which I did. Those evenings, that time of the day, were my most cherished.

Once beneath the covers, we were faster. Our bodies remained covetous—they did not hesitate. Afterwards he would place his head on my chest or stomach as we listened to our breath slowing, falling asleep immediately only to wake in the early hours to the beams of headlights across the ceiling.

In the morning, I'd find pieces of dried plaster on my sheets after he'd left. He liked to eat apples in the shower, so I began keeping a bag on my bedside table. He left their browning cores in the sink, which I found gruesome, but there they were, anyway, his presence. And always there was my instrument waiting in the corner. Sometimes I crossed over to it seamlessly, other times I could not find their convergence: the cello player and the lover.

The composer introduced me to the music video for Meredith Monk's song, *Turtle Dreams*, when I was younger. In it, Monk dances as one of four performers; there are two men and two women, dressed in black, moving against a bare, pink background. They sing this song, and it contains barely any lyrics. The only discernible lines are variants of, *I went to the store*, and apart from that, what they vocalise is nonsense. The extension of their voices, their range, nonetheless contains an emotion that seems to move beyond the bounds of what the written word is capable; they wail and shriek, like sirens sometimes, their voices getting away from each other, wild and isolated, before returning to harmony.

The music accompanying the vocals is a waltz, played on an organ. The singers move in pairs, in time to this music, their postures unbending, which feels familiar, like folk dancing. Except it isn't familiar. It seems there is something restrained beneath the artfulness of the video's staging, some insolence, maybe, in their faces. Yet they are not really speaking. It is not clear if they do not have the language, or they are choosing not to use it.

Towards the end, Monk turns her back to the viewer, and the three other performers, to look at something upstage. We do not know what's caught her attention, what causes this distance between her and the audience. She is brought back eventually by her male partner; they perform a tender dance during which he appears to reason with her, and she does not fight him. Perhaps she does not know what to say. All four of them seem to understand their positions and what is expected of them, alone and together. I wonder, how do they know that?

The film hasn't always made me think of romance, although it is, in many ways, romantic. Often, it has made me think of militancy. The point seems to be that they're dancing, and they're singing, and it's all faintly domestic, but at certain moments, and at the same time, they're also screaming. I think the composer wanted to show me something about the voice through this, how far it can be pushed, how it can be a mutiny. But, for me, it's also about the voice's limitations.

If Billy seemed shy, or uncertain, in the beginning, it wasn't the entire story. His father had abandoned him and his mum just after he was born, and when we spoke about this, which was rarely, I glimpsed a more strident side to him. He was dismissive, scornful about his father. His room in his mum's flat only had a single bed, so we didn't stay much, but when we did, I noticed how protective he was of her, how he pre-empted her movements, how he acted, in many ways, like her partner. I mentioned this one morning after we'd slept there, and he said,

'Right. Yeah, it's embarrassing.'

Which surprised me.

'Is it?'

We were in his room gathering our stuff, and he started putting his shoes on without replying.

'I meant it seems nice to be so close,' I added.

'Would you want to be that close to your mum?'

I pulled a face, but he wouldn't smile, and the conversation seemed over. We left the flat and didn't discuss his parents any further. I felt stopped from pursuing the topic by something, and I could always sense this same stoppage in him whenever his father was mentioned. It was where the sense of Billy's stridency came from. And I wanted to know what it was, exactly—what he was refusing.

It was so difficult to find days I could sit for him that we'd still only managed one more for the sculpture he was making, and he claimed to need another before the studies were finished. The piece felt increasingly significant. He'd become more fixated, and this fixation had grown after attending my performance.

I was becoming aware that my concentration was suffering. No one else had yet noticed this, but Billy was on my mind even when I wasn't aware of thinking about him. I was turned towards the rest of the world, away from my instrument. This led to some nasty exchanges with the quartet's lead violinist, who was angry, also, about my solo work taking precedence. The second time I sat for Billy, we were interrupted constantly by my phone ringing, and every time I came back into his studio from the hallway, Billy would have his back to me. He would be doing something in the corner, would only turn around once I was back where he'd specified. We did not speak until the end of the session, when he explained it had not gone well, the distractions, obviously, were difficult.

'You could've switched it off,' he said, 'I know what you'll say, but you could easily have switched it off.'

He was right, of course. The problem was I hadn't wanted to. It was my career. I needed my phone on.

'I've still been here,' I said. 'Don't take that away.'

'But you weren't. You just kept leaving.'

Now, I wonder if it wasn't also, in part, his anger fuelling the creation of that sculpture.

Anger was what I, too, was feeling. I was often waking in the night, when the dark was at its fullest, and if Billy was there, I would be forced to lie in bed running through compositions in my mind, resentful of his body beside me, until he woke, and then I wouldn't want him to leave. If he wasn't there, I would get up and practise, and my mind would be calm for a moment.

I was soon to perform the composer's new work at a venue in Philadelphia. Through the composer I had been introduced to a famous video artist, who'd asked me to perform a musical interpretation of his work, being staged by an important venue at the end of the following spring. The music was to be transcriptions of famous electronic pieces. The artist told me he wanted the cello because of how close its voice sounds to our own, and then he spoke about what I would be translating for him. His way of working, even his manner of speaking, was alien, and it took me a while to interpret his emails. My schedule was becoming frantic, but I found myself so doubting the language I used to speak to this man that I spent hours re-drafting messages that should have taken minutes. Perhaps it was also because Billy liked his work and had become excited when I told him about the performance.

For a month or so I had found myself crying, unexpectedly, in the shower, a few mornings each week. Afterwards I would dry my skin and forget about it, but I was turning thirty, and I was not yet, in my mind, the musician I wanted to be. Some permission was still, I sensed, being withheld, which I understood when I wasn't experiencing cohesion, when parts of my body—muscles, joints—acted up, distracted or disturbed me whilst playing, when I fluffed a note or when the music did not convey what I desired, when life merely felt like the forcing together of disparate moments. I had to be better, and it was always this fact I returned to. Although he was making no money from it and working mainly in removals, I knew Billy was a sculptor. But I was not yet a cellist.

Then Billy was asked to exhibit in a large group show. It was to take place in the spring. Although he didn't say so immediately, I gathered from his tone, the way he paced back and forth across my bedroom as he spoke, that it was important, perhaps the beginning of other things. Or, at least, that was what he was hoping.

Shortly after this news, we went together to my parents' house. This wasn't the first time Billy had met them, but that time had been brief, so this was when my mother was first able to question him, which she did, at the dinner table. She had her legs tucked beneath her, seeming half risen from her chair, and she fiddled absentmindedly with things as she inquired how his sculpting was going. He explained about the group show, how he was working on pieces for it. She asked further about his practice—why he'd chosen sculpture over painting.

'I'm not sure,' he said, 'but there's only one way to view a painting, and with sculpture there are so many more angles.'

'And how do you know when you're finished?'

'I don't know if I'm finished.'

I waited for him to continue speaking, after he said this, expecting him to add something further, and when he didn't, there was an uneasiness. My mother and

I had both stopped eating, and then, after a moment, we looked at each other. I looked away quickly. What he'd said seemed insufficient for what he meant. Perhaps what I felt was apprehension, and this might have been because of my mother, but it might also have been because of the group show, in which he was intending to use the sculpture he was making based on the studies of my body. I didn't want to be presented as a thing that was unfinished even though that was what I was.

My mother had also, perhaps, expected him to keep speaking as she didn't ask another question. I wanted to know what she was thinking. *What does it mean?* I wanted to ask her, but I couldn't. I knew I wouldn't ask even when I next saw her, alone, because it would allow her a power I didn't want to offer. He was mine, and I wanted to demonstrate this in everything. At many points that evening, I might even have placed a hand on him, coming in between them, not that she would have cared or noticed. So, why did I do it?

My dad started asking Billy about his mum, after he'd mentioned living with her, and then my mother interrupted to ask about his father, if Billy was close with him. I hadn't told them about his father.

'He left us,' Billy replied. 'I hate him, to be honest. We barely speak.'

My mother leant forward, her face concentrated, and then she asked, in her usual way, if hate was really what he meant, if it wasn't something more complex.

'It's what I mean,' he said.

And it really was, I thought. The sense of refusal, which I felt when he spoke about his father, was present, but in that context, it seemed about privacy. It felt correct. This was something I'd never been able to do in the face of her questioning. He didn't say anything further, and she didn't ask again.

His group show became a thing after that. An event towards which his entire life was directed. It was the first time I'd experienced him having this focus, and it was both a comfort and not a comfort at all that an image of my body was at its centre. I worried about this body. I did not know it.

It must've been around this time that he came to see one of my performances with the quartet. He was sat behind a very tall man in the audience, and for the entire concert I could see Billy's head, the stage lights catching it hazily, craned awkwardly over this man's shoulder. He did this to watch me on the right-hand side of the stage, and I remember this: every single head in the auditorium facing the same way but for one, at a funny angle.

As our relationship became more established, I kept expecting to come suddenly to annoyance or disillusion, as others had warned me happened over time with love. When I didn't, it was through this I understood something about the seriousness of my feelings, which was that they appeared to be permanent. This was unsettling. Yet it was not the only narrative I was enthralled to. There must have been another narrative, because what trick of mind made me feel I was always on the verge of losing him? Did I fear losing him because I knew how hard it was to retain our commitment, how close I got to abandoning things?

Often there was a sort of soreness to proceedings. One Saturday night, I returned from a performance in Berlin with my body aching so badly I was unable to lift my bag into the plane's overhead locker. Billy had promised he'd come over after going to the pub with someone he disliked but felt obliged to spend time with. This type of pretence frustrated me, but he was careful with people, not like me. I had not seen him for quite a few days, and I wanted to see him. He texted around midnight to say another of his friends had appeared and wanted him to stay, there was a spare ticket to a club night, and he hadn't seen this friend in ages, so he was going. He said he hoped that was alright, which, really, it wasn't, but I didn't know how to translate my desire into the necessary words. My desires were selfish, and

I didn't want to appear selfish, so I replied with something terse, which he misread as agreement, and my bed felt even more lonely.

I awoke to find he'd not sent any further texts, and when I called, he did not answer. I seemed to roll a little, off the world's axis. I spent all day crying, unable to eat, drinking cans of coke. I had no idea what was happening. I laughed at my puffy, woeful face in the mirror.

I couldn't seem to locate the source of my misery: what Billy had done was not terrible, and I would see him that evening. It occurred to me I might just miss him, which seemed absurd, but there it was anyway. I had never before needed someone like that.

I took a shower and emerged to find a voicemail from him, just as the sun was sinking. He was on his way over. When he arrived, my hair was wet, my room was filled with the orange light of an early dusk. He told me he'd been sleeping; he'd gone to his studio at three in the morning whilst he was still high, and it had gone badly. He'd been overcome with doubts about the show, which seemed even more important since he'd learnt certain galleries would be attending. It had felt, he said, like there was nothing in his studio that mattered.

I heard him say this whilst also knowing there was a reproduction of my own body in there, so I asked explicitly about that piece, for clarity, and he told me it was wrong, there was something wrong in it. I could see what he was saying. I knew in one sense it was part of the process, that things had to be wholly bad before they became in any way good, but I was also startled by this wrongness, which seemed to reside in my own body, to lie between us. I was wounded by what he was saying.

At the time, I was not aware he'd been in contact with his father. I'd assumed he had little interest in them speaking, and I did not know how long the desire to do this had occupied him.

Arriving at his studio late one evening, I found him pacing. He handed me a sheet of lined paper and explained it was a reply that his father had sent to a letter he'd posted six weeks earlier. It was torn from a notebook. It was written in large, messy letters, in blue biro, with faint indentations of other words on top of those written, which must've been from the sheet of paper above in the notebook. What I can remember is that it was shocking. It contained a threat to harm Billy, the actual words of which escape me, and when I asked what he'd sent to receive such vitriol, he told me nothing, a sentence, some mention of the group show. He'd wanted to let his father know.

'It was an invitation,' he said, not looking at me or the letter. 'I wanted to say something, and the show felt like a reason.'

An invitation. I considered whether this was really the extent of it. It seemed clear he wasn't lying, he was not deceitful, but I found myself wondering, rather, if he might have omitted something without being aware of doing so. I was surprised he wanted to speak to this man in the first place. I realised he must have already sent his letter when we had dinner with my parents, when he'd stated his hatred so assuredly.

He told me he'd discovered his father's address, in Andalusia, where he'd retreated many years earlier, but, at first, he'd hesitated to write because he didn't want to be misinterpreted.

'I didn't want it to be wrong. I didn't want to allow him anything, and words always seem a bit wrong,' he said. 'A bit fabricated.'

I had told him before I felt something similar with my mother. Her work was studying the parts of reality that didn't really exist, and my words would often disintegrate beneath her scrutiny, until my sentences began to feel hollow, and my beliefs, my feelings, as empty as them. I knew the distressing thing about this was not knowing when, or how, you'd gone wrong in the first place.

'I decided to send one sentence,' he said, 'in the end, to see if he would reply.'

'But you couldn't have wanted him at the show, really?' I said, gripping the letter, not wanting to give it back. Not wanting him to read the threat again.

'I don't know. I want something. I wish I didn't.'

He took hold of the paper in one corner and stood next to me.

'Can you see the indents?' he said, tracing them with his finger. 'Don't they look like another letter? An earlier draft of this one?'

If it was an earlier draft, the content of the letter had changed between the two versions. There were many more words in the previous one, and the handwriting was more careful, but it was impossible to decipher the words. I saw him looking at these indentions with loathing and desperation, and I felt pained by the idea he was clinging to. I still feel pained by it. The suspicion that, somehow, he could've made things better.

That same month, I went for dinner with a childhood friend, who was an English teacher. We were eating spaghetti in an Italian restaurant, and she told me she was to have a hysterectomy. She had endometriosis, she explained, which had become too widespread for the doctors to treat. She'd been experiencing pain for years without knowing the reason—and that the pain was caused by something bigger was strange. It had come to seem ordinary, to be expected. She said she'd gone to get the results of her initial keyhole surgery, when she was told how serious the endometriosis was, and afterwards had become lost in the hospital.

It was large and the pathways between the departments were convoluted in a way that seemed, to her mind, deliberate. She told me she walked down these corridors, at first trying to follow signs, in the end abandoning them to follow her instinct in an attempt to find the waiting area, where she'd left her sister. The corridors were hot and windowless, and she felt unwilling to ask a nurse for directions, though she passed many. After twenty minutes or so she realised what she was waiting for: she wanted to be called over the system. She told me that it was so simple she laughed. She wanted to hear her name called out.

'And was it?'

'In the end,' she said. 'It didn't change anything.'

The corridors were still maze-like, the waiting area still undiscoverable. Her name didn't tell her where she was. It didn't tell her anything.

When she did ask a nurse, she was taken to another waiting area, identical but with different coloured chairs, and she had to sit there and phone her sister. She was incapable of searching any longer.

The funny thing, she said, in the restaurant, sounding calmer than her story suggested, was that she already knew she couldn't have children: the endometriosis had done too much damage. Yet it had still taken her ages to book the hysterectomy. It turned out her womb wasn't so easy to abandon. She guessed no body part would be.

'I feel I need it all very much. It's all mine and perhaps I need every bit,' she said.

She didn't know what made her who she was—that was what she was telling me. And what idle thread might she pull, I thought, which could end up unravelling everything?

When I went to Philadelphia, with the composer, the city was bright and neat, and it was a relief to walk the long, straight avenues alone each morning, when I could not sleep because of my jet lag. Before my last performance I voiced something to myself, out loud, which I'd never done before. I told myself I was terrified. Why I felt the need to say this, I do not know, but during that performance I was more aware than usual of the seats rising to the ceiling, the faces of the audience lined up endlessly behind each other. Looking at them, I had the impression of puppets, moving gently, peering up at the stage, clapping, expectant and unreachable.

I felt my falseness. I had voiced my fright, allowed it in, made it actual. It was as if my words were there, in the dark beyond the spotlights, like creatures, waiting patiently.

In Philadelphia's Museum of Art there was a painting by Dorothea Tanning. It contained a woman, perhaps the artist, in the foreground, with a small monster-like creature at her feet. Her own monster, I would say. Behind her were a series of partially open doors. The woman was topless, and she was looking knowingly out of the painting, seemingly aware of its artifice. The question that came to my mind was: who might walk through all those doors?

I sent a postcard of the painting home to the teacher, who was recovering from her operation, and I also brought one back for Billy, which I wrote something brief and probably too earnest on, and it's possible he still has this postcard, that maybe he still looks at it, turns it in his hand, notes the fading ink, but it doesn't change the fact I can't remember what I wrote to him.

When we saw each other on my return, we went on a canal boat with his friends. We had spoken nearly every day whilst I'd been in America, but our physical distance had seemed to infect our conversations, leaving them muted. I would be tired after a day of rehearsal, and he'd be about to sleep, so our voices would often trail off, leaving thoughts or feelings unexamined. It had been difficult to grapple with the size of these issues, or the hurt he felt over his father. I had just wanted him closer, and when I'd told him that, his voice had become clearer—he'd agreed, he'd wanted me.

On my return, we sat towards the front of the canal boat in between the belongings of the others, and I spoke about Philadelphia. I was explaining how eerie I'd found the stage, which had struck me for the first time like a body of black water. I tried to explain to him my impression of the puppet-like people, but as I spoke, my voice sounded unnatural. With every attempt to make it sound normal, it became more affected. I described the size of the stage several times, and then, also, the height of all the buildings, how wide the hotel bed seemed, how bad my relations with the quartet were, the excitement of the composer, who'd decided to extend the project into an album. It was a great tangle, I explained, yet everywhere I looked was distance. I could not find a sense, in the middle, of what mattered. This was what I was trying to tell him, but something in his eyes made me suspect the distance I'd felt in America had returned with me. And suddenly his mouth was twisted.

'Are you boasting?' he said.

It took me a second to understand him.

'About America?' I replied.

He shook his head.

'It doesn't matter.'

We sat in silence as the others called between themselves. I knew he'd been struggling with his work after receiving his father's letter, that he was still angry. A part of me wanted to know more about this anger and a part wanted to deny its existence—it was too ungainly.

'Is your work still not going well?' I said, quietly.

'That's not what I was talking about. When I said that.' He stood up. 'Don't make me sound jealous.'

He walked over to the roof, so I was left alone at the front of the boat, staring out over the water. I did not want to turn around and watch him talk, playfully, with the others. I had been trying to speak about the proportions of things, their textures, and I was surprised by how completely he'd misunderstood me. We were listening to Julius Eastman's *The Holy Presence of Joan D'Arc*, and, as its riff repeated, I went back over what I'd said, trying to make sense of Billy's reaction. But I wasn't sure about everything I'd said, or how carefully he'd been listening.

He crouched at the front of the boat as we approached the tunnel that led to King's Cross. Its opening, waiting in a brick wall, was small and entirely black inside. The completeness of this made it feel like a living thing, which we were foolish to enter. Billy's friend handed him a torch. He was right at the stern, so he entered the darkness a few seconds ahead of me. I watched it come over his body, bit by bit, his face turned back momentarily, the last piece of him in the light before it too was subsumed to the tunnel. The place smelt stagnant, and I was aware of the water's lapping presence, at the sides of the boat beneath the music, which continued. The same notes, sequences, adding onto each other.

He turned back, shining the torch in my direction, and the light hit me all at once. I had to close my eyes. He said,

'Are you alright?'

But I could not open my eyelids because the light was blinding, which I felt he must realise.

Behind them, on the inside, I could see veins and blood vessels in their massed patterns, and I could not look away from them, could not open my eyes, because the light did not leave me. In those patterns I saw an image. It was of my friend's uterus in a clean, silver dish, left alone on a table, in a large operating theatre, whilst around it, men and women moved at a distance. It was red, still, and contained the heat of her. It had been taken whilst she slept. But it was growing colder as it sat there. It was an ugly thing. And once her, I thought. It was once her, as much as her eyes or her head. I wondered, in that tunnel, what they could possibly have done with it.

*

In the morning the sky was steely, and it felt like we were trapped inside something. I told him it wasn't fair to talk to me like that when we were with his friends, and I was alone among them. But he would not allow that word *alone*.

'Were you not with me?'

'You know what I'm saying.'

'If alone was what you felt, it must have been what you wanted.'

I could not catch at the thread of this argument, which he seemed to wind around me. I had wanted to keep things clear, precise, but it was as if he intentionally chose to muddle things.

'You have to explain to me how I offended you, because I can't make it out,' I said.

'You didn't *offend* me.'

'So, what, I was insensitive?'

'What do you want from me, a life, or what?'

'A life. Of course. Isn't that what anyone wants?'

He explained then that strangers in America wanted to see me and even his father didn't want to see him, and so I saw more of what his hurt was about, and yet I still felt it had no bearing on what I'd been trying to explain on the canal boat. What I'd been trying to explain was that I was also unsure of things.

'I can't work,' he said. 'I can't focus. And I don't always believe you, when you say you want the same things.'

I asked if he was blaming me for his difficulties, perhaps because often when the same happened to me, I blamed him. But he grew defensive. It wasn't what he was saying, he accused me of a slyness in suggesting this.

'Why would I be sly? I'm trying to understand you.'

'Stop holding yourself outside the argument then. It's as if I'm not your problem.'

'What do you want me to do?'

'You could sacrifice things, just a little.'

'And what sort of sacrifice would be acceptable?' He turned his face away, so I knew a sacrifice was in his mind, but he was not ready to reveal it. 'You didn't want me to go to Philadelphia?'

'I wanted you to go. I want you to be successful. I just want to feel a part of things and I've told you that. I can't explain it better. I know how it sounds. I know it's selfish.'

'I want to be part of your work too.'

'But you are,' he said. 'You're literally what I'm working on. You're always on my mind. It's maddening.'

'So, can't you allow the same for me?'

'What you do is different. I'm not performing.'

I could sense him calming down, and perhaps this is why I left the comment. I knew he was wrong in what he said, but to say this would've been to cause more rupture: to point out his performance was his identity, to point out my performance was also a creation I tended in private.

The Julius Eastman composition we listened to on the canal boat is atonal. It contains a high level of dissonance, is unpredictable. It was written for cello ensemble—ten cellos begin by playing the same riff together, and from there some stay with the riff whilst others move into counterpoint: following differing lines but remaining harmonically related.

The original manuscript for the piece became lost after Eastman was evicted from his home after falling into drug use, which ended his life not long after. He had achieved a level of success in New York's avant-garde scene of the eighties, but he had also faced homophobia and racism. The piece was reconstructed through a recording from the original. And it is both true that it is a work of genius, and that it is not easy to listen to.

This is the thing: the emotion of the harmonies and the rigidity of the repetition exist separately, but they are simultaneous, and neither gets away from the other. There is a desire for freedom, and a desire for order. I do not know if one becomes stronger—sometimes the two aspects seem to struggle, sometimes not. I have to let go of the urge for resolution whilst listening, so briefly I find it seems possible not to be one thing over another, to remain conflicted. It is not meant to be easy.

The music stays in the hard places it chooses.

In the week before his show opened, I found a model of myself in Billy's studio. The model was in the dark, in the corner, like a small, domesticated animal. He gave me the model when I asked, and although it did not look like me, it felt familiar. I knew this was the body I'd worried about.

I had come to his studio after a rehearsal with the video artist, which had run late, and I was feeling untidy, unsure, too aware of the opportunity the performance offered, the size of the audience being presented. I'd come to Billy for respite, and I wanted to take the model home. I wanted to own an object of his, to keep something with me of that refuge, and although I was scared to admit this—scared it might be misinterpreted as vanity—I asked for the model because it seemed, suddenly, imperative. He said I could do that. I could keep it.

I had told him, months before, that I could not share all of my space, and that my practice had to precede him. But at that point I could see the fallacy in this thinking, as if the different spaces of my life weren't always contracting and expanding, eating away at each other. I worried I was somehow making myself less serious by being with him, easing myself out of a strictness to welcome in more conventional modes of living, comforts. Yet I could not work out the situation we were in, what its boundaries were. There was a rhythm, but it never felt certain, and it didn't feel comfortable at all, and it did not seem to have conventions.

The private view for his show took place on a Thursday. This was the first show of his I'd been to, and I was unclear what it would be like, as an experience, though I was excited to be there with him, to witness him in that setting. But I didn't know if there would be a place for me, if I would feel welcomed. I walked into the gallery alone because I'd come from a rehearsal with the video artist, and Billy had needed to get there early. It was crowded. I saw him right away, in the middle of the room, stood a few metres away from his two sculptures, so that his relationship to them seemed vague. He was speaking with a shorter man, leaning back slightly, holding a beer but not drinking any, looking handsome.

Although the sculptures were in the middle of the room, which is where he'd told me they'd be, I couldn't see them properly due to the amount of people there. I could see people staring at them, but I could not see the sculptures. They seemed to be getting a lot of attention. Certainly, more attention than some of the paintings, which I spent a while viewing, in places where it was emptier. Many of the paintings were boring. I wanted to look at his sculptures.

Although I could've, I didn't try and speak to him. I knew it would be better for him to approach me, so that I could prove I was comfortable being alone, allowing him this moment in the spotlight. I felt I owed him this after all the times he'd come to my performances. I focused myself, instead, on his sculptures, trying to inch my way forward, towards them, but I found there were always new people coming in and leaving, and the crowd would not give me a clear view, so, instead, I walked around the outskirts of the room. I wasn't sure if he'd seen me, perhaps he had, but maybe he enjoyed being observed at the centre of things, and he, of course, did feel to me like the centre. I saw him this way from many angles. Occasionally one of his friends would spot me, and we'd make light conversation before moving away from each other in the general motion of the room, which seemed unending. This lightness suited me. I was restless, my palms were sweating.

Perhaps I was excited to see the piece I'd sat for, the larger form of the model he'd given me, *my* model, as I'd begun to think of it. I hadn't seen the sculpture because he hadn't wanted to show me before it was finished. Possibly, I was nervous, too, of seeing it and of the crowd, which seemed loud and opinionated.

When I approached the sculptures again, a space cleared, which I slipped into, as if I were slipping through a narrow doorway. Once there, I did not have the space to turn around, so the sculpture of my body was the only thing I could see, its figure. I was aware that from where he stood, Billy, if he chose to look, would be able to see me in this position, but I didn't turn to check if he was doing so. The sculpture was bigger than I'd anticipated. I'd assumed it would be life size, but it was just slightly larger. It was substantially larger than my clay model. The piece was recognisable from the model, but only just, and in many ways the sculpture was completely different.

There was something distressing about its form. The lines were human, but the shapes they made were less familiar. I was unclear what was being arrived at. It did not look like me, it was entirely abstract, distorted, and yet I worried that, from it, I might be recognisable to other people in the gallery. I felt as if I was standing there stripped, naked.

He'd named the sculpture *First Movement* and perhaps that was partly the problem—the growth implied in the title, how it seemed to take on many forms at once. The way it was many things made it seem living, and the way it was living, but not inhabited, made it feel deathly. Because it was not quite human, there was no safe space I could rest my eyes on, not a limb, or a finger, or an ear lobe—no itemisation. No distinctions. It was too whole, too present. I did not like it. I looked it over again, closed my eyes, opened them, and still, I did not like its presence. Perhaps I was disappointed, perhaps I'd expected something more beautiful, but I was in many ways repulsed by the sculpture.

Was it how he saw me? This was something I could not ask because it was simplistic, foolish even. It was not the point. The sculpture was not me, but still I wanted to ask this question. He'd said I was always in his mind, and so, in his mind, was this what I seemed like? I turned away from the sculpture. I had to push past a few people to be out of its vicinity. I was aware again, for the first time since I'd managed to get there, of Billy being able to see me, and as I walked away, my face hot, I felt sure he'd been watching.

I return to fear, like returning to my body after sleeping. I find, unavoidably, the question of femaleness with this, because I would like to know where the fear resides, be it my arm, my leg, be it in some part concealed: a part of my body I've never regarded. I would like to know, because then I could make a correction. I could change my posture, alter the balance, play it better.

The day of the video artist's opening performance arrived with clouds, a grey of varied hues rising solemnly over the city. It became sunnier in the afternoon, and on my way to the performance, there was a light that felt like summer, although it was only April. Billy had been busy at the group show for the last fortnight, but he was going to be there that evening, as was the composer. I hadn't let my parents come because I did not need further pressure. When I arrived backstage, I was on the phone to Billy. He said I seemed calm, happy. He heard me say hello to the artist. I can't remember this. I do not have any memories of strange events that with hindsight become revelatory.

I can remember little, either, of the actual performance. Because various people were there, and many people heard about what happened afterwards, I have had accounts from more people than I care to recall. What I was told by either Billy, or the composer, was that it happened about fifteen minutes into the first half. I was alone on the stage. Because they described my movements, I can see all of these, I can hear the music. Neither of them described my face, so in the memory I am faceless. Sometimes this disturbs me but not always. Sometimes I think, if only I had been faceless, unrecognisable.

The composer said I was moving uncharacteristically, as if I was distracted. That I seemed to be having trouble with my fingerings. He claimed I wasn't off by much, or at least most of the audience wouldn't have noticed, but there were one or two false notes, and I wouldn't stop looking at my hands, he said, which was bizarre. But perhaps Billy said that. He told me my hands looked like they were cramping, my bow was shaking. Then, abruptly, it was as if I threw it away. I remember him saying, I threw it from my body.

'It was like you didn't want it anywhere near you,' he said. 'Like you were disgusted.'

He told me my neck went entirely red, a terrible bruised red, then this spread to my face, and it became clear I was having trouble breathing.

When that was obvious, Billy got up from his seat and started trying to reach the aisle, but this took a long time because the rows were so long. A lot of people must've thought my actions were part of the performance, which was surreal anyway, but he knew they were not—this was not anything I would have done to myself. He was stumbling over bags and legs, he said, and then, before he got to the aisle, I was on the floor, on my hands and knees, my cello dropped, the curtain immediately down, a noise like he'd never heard rising from the audience—suddenly lit again. A swelling sound of fear and excitement.

'They couldn't believe it,' he said, 'they were demanding the curtain back up.'

The composer told me he caught up to Billy in the aisle, and as the audience began to rise, they made their way through the bodies to the backstage area where they had an argument with a stagehand who would at first only allow the composer back there, before relenting. It was empty but for a few bodies passing quickly to the stage in black outfits. They found me still on the stage, surrounded by a group of organisers, my agent, the video artist. It was clear the panic attack wasn't over, and they all waited, Billy unable to get closer because a pair of women had taken charge without seeming to agree on a course of action.

There were many requests for a paper bag to help with my breathing, and either no one went to fetch one, or someone did but returned empty handed, or with a plastic bag that was no use. Someone debated the use of a paper bag in the first place. Glasses of water, a towel, painkillers, a bar of chocolate—these things were passed around the group endlessly, but were left undrunk, unused. At their feet I was choking.

A medic or a doctor appeared, pushing through the group, and Billy took the opportunity to follow him. The women had decided to get me moving, so they'd dragged me up by my arms, and he had to get hold of me. I remember them all being furious, bearing down on me, but he said this was not the case, not then, not immediately after in the surreal atmosphere of the stage, listening to the roaring sound of the audience on the other side of the curtain. He told me no one had been angry.

It is difficult with these accounts to determine if I can remember anything of my own. I believe I can remember noticing how white my hands seemed beneath the lights, and below them only the dark of the stage, which seemed like a great expanse of empty space through which I was falling. I seem to have had a realisation of death in this, and then the death came to my body.

And someone was standing. I see my hands, then look out past the lights and know something is wrong because someone is standing in the audience. A silhouette, tall among the seated. I want the person to sit down because if they do, it might not be the case that something is happening. The person standing up and the feeling of dying are interwoven, as if the person is causing the pain I am feeling. I want to ask what right they have to do this, but I can't find my breath, can't summon a note of resistance.

That must've been Billy, who stood up because he did not know what was happening, but he needed to get to me because he too might've believed I was dying. So that's who it is in my memory. But, of course, other people might've stood, it might've been a stranger.

There is a video on YouTube of Pablo Casals performing his most famous piece of music in an empty room beside a wall of large, rectangular windows. It must have been filmed half a century ago. It is grainy, sepia, but the way the light falls through the windows, the way the canopies of the trees beyond them waver, feels close, like it's happening now. The sunlight falls through the leaves onto bare ground, the leaves make shadow, and he plays his cello. I've watched this video hundreds of times, and always the trees and the light meet in this way, always he plays before them. I find the sound of his cello disturbs the time between us, so I am in that room, seeing the shadows on the dirt as it is warmed by the sunlight, glad to be within the white walls, protected.

I watched the video again, recently, after bumping into the flautist on the train. Something made me want the video's light, although it seemed slightly darker than I recalled, and in fact many parts of the video that I'd remembered clearly, fondly, were either not there or entirely altered. I'd believed at some point the camera panned away to reveal the other rooms of the house—a home I'd decided for some reason was Casals'—the spaces calm save for the movement of the leaves outside the windows and a sense of something happening nearby that might, any moment, invade them. But this did not happen. The camera panned once only to include the woman at the piano, and other than that it stayed with Casals. The other rooms, the house, were in my head. Yet when I think of the video, I keep picturing the home—its objects, his life within.

I believe I watch this video because I want to know how a man like that considers himself, as he bathes, eats, wakes in the morning, shields his eyes from the sunlight. Everywhere he goes, he must know he is something to others, and to himself, perhaps, much less of something. To himself nothing but warmth under a blanket, maybe, a mass of needs that cannot see itself but for indentations, which it leaves in cushions, mattresses. I wonder where his fear lives, whether he knows it only through the marks it leaves on a world he feels from a distance. The fact that Casals is dead does not change the way I think of him, how present he is in this story.

When I miss Billy, when the longing stretches beyond a few hours, and days are mislaid to the past, it feels like I'm searching for something sturdier than he ever managed. Something like an idea, which over time has clouded. I might be searching for the moment before the veil was lifted from my eyes. So, when I miss Billy, I watch this video. And it's in that dream of the world, the bright leaves shuffling beyond the window, that I find solace.

He moved in with me after that night. I was forced to cancel all my performances for two months, so that replacements or alternatives could be found, and other people would not be forced to work with the question mark I suddenly embodied. After a few conversations, the quartet decided another cellist would cover for me until the extent of the problem was known. In case of another *breakdown*, the lead violinist told me on the phone.

That was his word, even though I'd told him it was a panic attack. He continued to use that word even after I corrected him, and many other people also used their own words to describe what had happened, but I did not recognise these words, could not tie them to myself.

I could see myself on that stage, choking, I could see myself next to Billy in bed, sedated, I could see myself on stage at another time, playing Elgar before an orchestra. These versions of myself were not unrelated, yet the nature of their relation became vague. How I got from one place to another, I could not say.

Billy had taken me to hospital that night, after the performance, when it became clear whatever was happening wasn't stopping on its own. After looking at several options, the doctor explained I was having a panic attack, or, more precisely, waves of them. In one sense I understood this. I knew panic attacks could be severe and disabling, yet in other ways I had no memory of panicking. I had not felt panicked, though Billy told me this was odd because I'd seemed it—I was still acting strangely, he added. To me, it was the situation producing the strangeness, but to him it was the other way around. That was another thing that was surprising. What would panic feel like? I asked myself this. It was a question that had seemed obvious, until it wasn't.

Then flowers began arriving. Some did not have cards, or the names on the cards were unreadable. I had the impression they'd come from nowhere, but they established themselves in my bedroom, so that it quickly became a different place than the room I'd practised in for the weeks before the concert. That room was the past, the flowers the present. I usually received flowers after a performance, but these flowers were different. Their colours were subdued. They were tasteful, solemn. My cello, which had been damaged when I'd dropped it, was with my luthier, and the flowers were in my bedroom, dropping their petals. *But no one has died*, I kept saying to myself, when more flowers started arriving. I repeated it like a mantra. Yet the situation had changed. This was what I needed to admit.

For the first few weeks my time was filled by having this explained to me, or by explaining it, in turn, to others. When I explained to others all I did was repeat what had been explained to me, but I did so with assurance, as if I was the one to have understood things. I knew the facts. People believed something must've happened to cause such an episode. Many people asked about Billy, perhaps we'd had a fight, they offered, as if I wouldn't remember, or as if a fight with Billy might cause me to abandon all my ambitions. No, I explained. Nothing happened. I'd slept, I'd eaten. I said this all with that cool assurance, but, really, I had no faith in the details. The details were bits of detritus blowing past me in a harsh wind.

Money made the decision for Billy to move in simple, but for me this decision was easy for other reasons. Our relationship, suddenly, had to be a given.

The day my cello arrived home from the luthiers Billy opened the door because I showed no sign of moving. I went to the landing and listened to him carry it up the stairs slowly, as if he was unsure which way to hold it, and possibly scared of more damage, but I went back into my room before he turned the corner, so he did not see me.

He asked where it would go. Its usual corner was full of his belongings, so we tried the other corner, but I was worried by the closeness of the radiator. He stood holding it in the middle of the room for a long time as I considered other places, knowing, really, I wanted it under my bed, yet realising that sounded foolish. Would it fit under the bed? I asked him this, but he said it wouldn't. In the end, I moved his things over to the other corner, and the cello went where it always had, on its side, surrounded by piles of sheet music.

It was awkward with the cello in the room. I didn't want Billy to catch me looking at it, so I avoided doing so when he was there, and he also avoided that corner. I threw the old flowers away, but some of the petals left pollen marks on the rug, so the smell lingered. I found it deathly. When Billy wasn't around, I took the cello and tried to play the music I had been meant to perform that night, so I might remember what had happened, what had made me panic, but a fog had gathered. I couldn't play it. Even with the sheet music in front of me, I found it impossible. It was as if the notes were missing.

The night my cello came home, Billy washed my hair. I had not washed it since the concert, so he suggested he might help. I did not want help, did not see the point in washing, but he told me, gently, I smelt damp, like soil, too earthy. It seemed strange, difficult, that I might smell this way.

'What happened?' I asked, turning on him in the bath, shampoo down my face. 'Why did that happen to me?'

I went to a counsellor. My old professor found me someone who had experience with what she called *stage frights*, which was another term people were using, although she was the only one who used the plural. I couldn't be bothered to correct her. The counsellor asked if I'd ever been scared before, but I didn't understand the relevance. Of course, I'd been scared before. I didn't remember being scared then, on that stage. I remembered anticipation. She noted this word down whilst I sat watching.

It felt, I told her, like I'd been on a bright, speeding train, heading happily towards a destination, only for that train to stop in the middle of nothing—a field somewhere—and for the lights to go off, but for no one to explain why it had happened. Not to know if it might begin again. And I was standing in that field, alone, where the grass was long, staring at the unlit train, willing it to revive itself, because I had no other means to get anywhere.

She asked about that word *happily*. She asked me to say what it meant to head 'happily' somewhere, so I narrowed my eyes and said: *with purpose*.

My parents hadn't been at the performance. It was difficult for my dad to grasp the severity of what had happened; without the spectacle it could be made to sound normal, a case of nerves maybe. Sitting around their kitchen table, he wanted to know the reason for cancelling everything. I tried to explain, pulling out sentences I'd used with other people, the sentences my agent had used, sentences that didn't satisfy my father.

'It's because they don't trust her,' my mother said, finally, 'they no longer believe she's a certainty.'

It was exactly the problem. Yet I couldn't stand to hear it, so blunt, when I had been careful to imbed my language with vagueness.

'But I am certain!' I cried, not knowing myself. I was breathless, and in my dad's face, I found my own: wounded, blinking.

Again, my mother was right, certainty was the issue. Without regaining my certainty, I did not see a way back to the stage. I knew, then, I had to consider the situation as an event that happened because I'd lost something. Yet I resisted considering it this way. I did not want to think of loss, which could, for all I knew, be permanent. I wanted that night to be an aberration, because I did not want to change any ideas of myself.

I needed to become better, but I did not know how to do this. In the mornings, as Billy got ready to go to his studio, I would watch him through the angle of the open door, my head turned on the mattress. I would watch him move back and forth, brushing his teeth, eating cereal, whilst I stayed where I was, having this view through an angle into a world, which seemed not to be mine any longer. I spent my days practising the pieces I was scheduled to perform even though the performances had been cancelled. The pieces sounded terrible, rushed, unsure, yet I kept playing them. I checked my emails obsessively to see if a venue might have suggested going ahead with a cancelled performance anyway—this seemed to be the easiest way out of the problem. I convinced myself I only needed one person to have faith in me, even though I knew I would never make it through a performance. Every time I was denied this solution by an empty inbox, I stumbled into extreme upset or anger. I could not believe it. I wanted to know who these people thought they were, taking so much from me.

'What right do they have to be so certain?' I asked Billy.

It was that night we went for dinner with the other cellist, though I could not eat, and the restaurant was too loud, and Billy had to speak for me. I was so glad for him being there. But I was so different in how I had been. And where was he in this?

There was the fact of him standing in the audience, the fact of his arms around me at the dinner table, the fact of the sculpture of which I'd felt so disgusted. These were things my mind went to without understanding their significance or order. They were my impressions of him. Yet he was different, his life was more than my thoughts. He was happy during this time, and I knew it then and it was difficult to understand, how he hid it from me, when I wanted to share in his excitement. He was in conversation with a gallery about representation, and he spoke to them in the bathroom if he had to speak to them at home, presumably because he thought I wouldn't be able to bear listening. This angered me, and yet he was right. It was difficult to handle. His success seemed inconsiderate.

I explained this to the counsellor, who at that point brought up the idea of grief, but *grief* sounded extreme. I had not lost anyone. She asked for how long I'd identified myself with my instrument, and I thought: was that what I'd done? It sounded trivial. I told her, there were no days on which I did not practise, no days I was without my cello. This was not about identification. It was just a fact—my voice came through it.

Then, nearly three months after that performance, Billy's father died in a plane crash. It was a small plane, containing only him and the pilot, who'd taken them to the centre of a storm for no good reason. Billy got the call at work. That evening he relayed the information: the plane had crashed in a valley close to his father's house, which was in the south of Spain, outside Seville. The pilot, who'd also died, was the owner of a bar near there, and he was believed to be reckless, had shown himself to be many times before. They'd been seen at this man's bar, drunk, in the morning. The bar had been recently redecorated, painted all over with pink gardenias, but I do not know why he was told this.

Over the next few days, I thought of this valley often. I sat in my flat, eating bits of bread and cheese, small biscuits. I had a picture in my mind of sparsity and lightning cutting the darkness of it, the silhouettes of trees seen in flashes. I imagined also the whistling sound a metal body would make, broken in half by the sky and falling through it. The storm, we understood, had come without warning, and yet the pilot must've seen something, I thought—a thickening grey, the assembly on the horizon.

I'd been having more attacks. They happened especially if I was doing anything strenuous, including speaking to the quartet or attempting to practise, and no doctor could discover what was wrong. When they came, they felt more like fits than anything. I had to cancel more performances. In fact, my agent decided we should cancel them all, and she diligently forwarded me emails from festivals and venues, expressing their concern, discussing potential to collaborate in the future. I had to reply to these, and the effort to do this felt strangely related to the effort I'd made to become the person they'd booked in the first place. It was like I was scratching out my own image, blanking out the details. And still I could not explain what happened. I was using terms other people had provided.

The news about the valley, the plane crash, came in the middle of this, and I found myself looking up the valley on the internet. I had started teaching the cello, as I had when I was younger, so I could make our rent, but I spent the hours I wasn't doing this, when Billy was at work or his studio, studying photographs of this place online, filled by a sense of falling.

A few weeks after we heard of the death, Billy was contacted by a solicitor in Seville. It turned out his father had left him everything, and, after a few moments of discussion with me, Billy booked a flight to Spain in a state of shock, to sort through the house and his father's belongings. The thought of doing this was bizarre to him: to touch this man's clothes, even his underwear, when he'd never been permitted anywhere near his body. He couldn't comprehend that his father, who'd been so angered by Billy's existence, so sure in this emotion, had really left him everything.

'But I don't feel sad,' he said. 'I can't feel anything.'

He went for a weekend, and we spoke several times a day, but before long, it was a week, and he lost his place at the removals company. There was something altered in his voice when we spoke. He told me the house was surrounded by dense vegetation, and he kept the windows open, so that everywhere he went in the house there was sound and motion: the leaves hissing on the bushes, the cicadas on the trees, the breeze moving through the rooms and hallways. He said this, and I was aware of being pulled. It was how I'd imagined the place, in all the hours I'd imagined it, but, also, I had in my mind that other house, the imagined home where Pablo Casals played his instrument.

Billy couldn't stay there longer because he didn't want to leave me alone. When he came back, he was slightly tanned, clear-eyed. He told me he wanted to move there. Of course, he wanted me with him. Even though in some part of my mind I must've been hoping to gain access to the home I had become so fixated on, I was not immediately keen on going. To go, I felt, would be a definitive act of abandonment towards my cello. Although I realised Billy would have to go—I could hear in everything he said the inevitability of this return, the relentlessness of the drive, the plea for resolution.

When he'd walked into the house, he told me, there'd been photographs lain all over the floor of the living room. They were old and new, in black and white, colour. They were in rows, and he'd wondered who might have done it before remembering he was the first one there, and so it must've been his father. Because of this, and the heat, the vertiginous effects of an early morning flight, he thought it might be a message—a story of some sort, to piece together.

He stared at them for days. The smells and sounds of the house were new to him, which meant he slept fitfully, and he didn't like to lie alone in a bed without me, on a mattress that held the indent of his father. He rose early to sit with the photos. He assumed they contained many of his relatives, and in some he found a hint of his appearance: he would stare at them until the faces started to betray a sense of animation, and for that moment he had it—all of his lineage, the past, the future—then they were still again, strangers with their hands to their mouths, hiding smiles, eyes furtive.

After a few days he went to the solicitor's office in Seville, and learnt, in fact, there'd been a mistake they blamed on mistranslation. His father hadn't meant to leave him anything because he hadn't made a will. Everything had passed to him by default. He took this silently, he told me, nodding as if it were information of little importance, but when he returned to the house, he was confronted again by the photos, and he realised among them were none of his mum, none of himself.

He swept all of them up and dumped them in a pile before the mantelpiece. And then he went around piling everything in the house into a large heap on top of them, in the middle of the vast room, chucking it together without reason, tearing things from walls or cupboards in the process, until the house was nearly bare but for this great heap of forsaken objects.

'I wanted it to burn,' he said, 'the whole pile. But, somehow, I couldn't do it.'

He told me, there were clothes and shoes, old razors, combs, books, pots and pans, which his father had cooked how many meals in? And I understood he was telling me it was a life, or its entrails: the hollowed presence of this man, evidence it was impossible for Billy to unsee, a life it was impossible to undo. The whole thing was too pitiful, he said, and he needed me to go back with him, so there could be more to life than just the endless accumulation of objects that will outlast you.

He told me he wanted a life for us, but there was no room in that flat in London, and there was no room for us within my despair. And when he said despair, I knew what he also meant was self-pity.

'I want you with me.' He said, under his breath, as if to himself.

The calmness with which he'd spoken was at odds with the propulsive nature of his feelings, how he'd torn the place apart once he'd realised his father had died failing him. I was wary of these feelings, of that house, the site of such alienation. I was wary of him wanting to return. Yet I also wanted to do this—I wanted to see that pile of objects he'd built at its centre, to see the house, the valley—why else had I spent so many hours studying it on the internet? I had this urge to witness its emptiness, which I could feel in Billy, how it was intimate.

'You could play there,' he said. 'It's all by itself. You'll get better because no one will be listening.'

I grew defensive at this formulation, the idea I had to get better. It was this thing I could not escape—that I had to acknowledge wrongness, touch it, muddy myself. I did not want to muddy myself.

'Do you think I need to get better?'

'I don't know—I can't understand the problem.'

He was very serious as he spoke, which made me realise he must've been contemplating my problem too, more than I'd realised. I imagined that pile of his, how long the dismantling of the house must've taken, what he must've felt to have seen everything together for the first time, all the sorrow.

He touched my hand.

'Don't make me go without you.'

I did not know who I'd be to turn from such love when it was offered. And he was right, my despair was taking up everything, and we had to be together.

Among some people, there was an idea I shouldn't go. Did I solicit these views or were they offered? My mother was the most forceful. She felt I should only do those things that originated within myself, that to follow, to put myself in that position, was foolish. I had lost so much already, she explained, it was reckless to give up more of my structures.

'Why foolish?' I said. I already felt like a fool, so it did not seem unwise to follow someone else's lead for once.

'You might not like it,' she said. 'It's not what you've done before.'

'Do you not like him?'

It had never occurred to me to ask this. It had never occurred to me someone might find him different than I did.

'What happens if your ability to perform doesn't return?'

'It will return.'

'You're sure then.'

I was not sure. My mother's concerns were my own, and yet hearing her voice them did what hearing her speak had always done—convinced me of the opposite.

'Relatively, yes.'

'But, going somewhere unknown—you see it might disturb you further?'

Was this my idea too? Whilst speaking to her I returned to the images of the bright plane breaking onto the dark landscape, the pile of belongings stacked high before a mantel, a sense of invasion, of a loss that has no context.

'That place will be his,' she said. 'And where will you be?'

I went to the composer's house a few days later, to find him among his rabbits. They'd become fat, and he'd grown thin. I told him about Spain, and he replied that the idea of living in such heat seemed like madness. Then he seemed to forget what he'd been saying and started telling me work for the album was going slowly because he could not decide upon things, kept re-imagining what he'd already done, picking it apart, dissecting. I asked what it was he wanted, if he knew, and he said, of course, it was intricacy.

'But there's no end point,' he said. 'Now, I just want the music to fulfil every expectation of the crowd whilst at the same time doing very little, almost nothing. As if all they might actually desire is one note, held perfectly.' He looked back at me, blinking as if to clear his eyes of something.

I asked him again what he thought of me going to Spain.

'Will it make you better?'

'I don't know.'

'The distance will be a nuisance when I need you.'

For the first time I doubted I'd be the one to perform his music, his perfect note, which did seem what the audience was often after: to hear just one good thing and then lose it, and through this know something more about the farce of things, the quickness. As I watched the composer, sitting there, thin and preoccupied, I wondered how it would feel to be with someone whose language I understood already.

I told him I couldn't play at all. I explained the issue, and he shook his head, grimacing as I kept speaking, when I grew more animated.

'But it was, from a certain viewpoint, an extraordinary performance,' he said, 'and I think it's a shame no one thought to mention that. It only failed in the established intentions. In other ways, it was far more exciting.'

During my final session with the counsellor, I mentioned Billy's sculpture. I asked if it had any bearing on me, if its existence was enough to cause some rupture. I explained it wasn't of me, but it was formed from my presence. She repeated that word, *formed,* then said another, *malfunction,* in the way she would repeat and offer many words without explanation, and then, again, she wanted to discuss my cello. She wanted to know how badly it had been broken. To what extent I'd injured it.

The idea of malfunction stayed with me, and I came to this suddenly: I was failing to be myself. It was this, not being myself, that must've been the cause of the breakdown. Somehow this simple figuration, so unresistant, made me feel better, even though it changed nothing. It gave me a route, which was not about going forward. I only had to go back on myself.

Was this the message of my mother? Was this what the composer meant, about the performance?

I made efforts. I saw friends, entered the world, accepted tickets to concerts. I played the music I'd performed already, although the sound was weaker, and the more I played these pieces, the more the sound thinned, as if it was eroding, until I could not play them anymore. I grew sick, weary. I went to Spain. I went to be with Billy.

I liked the house. This surprised me because in many ways it was an ugly building. It was larger than I'd realised, although badly kept, and the furniture, what was left, was cheap and flimsy. When the sun set, its light struck the back wall of the home and when the sun rose, it did the same to the front wall, casting the silhouette of a lemon tree onto the white stucco. The tree grew in the driveway. The white of the exterior walls felt clean and blank. It felt, when I stood outside, like a home for us. Inside, it did not always feel like a home of ours, but when I looked at the sun on the stucco walls, I could almost convince myself. Containment was what I wanted.

In the beginning, I believed playing my instrument, hour on hour, restating my commitment, would repair our bond. To contemplate fear seemed a sure way to feel it, and I did not want to feel fear, so I went every morning to my cello.

I must have been tired. I recall how my body moved then, and it moved as if it was exhausted. I heard no emotion in my music. It was piecemeal, the notes unrelated, no story building between them, my body unable, unwilling, to carry a passage to revelation. The mass of Billy's dad's belongings remained in the living room, and I could sense its pull wherever I went in that home. In comparison, my music was without presence. I played my repertoire and I hated it. I practised scales, tuned the instrument obsessively, tried again, and still I hated the sound I made. In the deadness of the notes, I heard panic. To hear it made me feel it—I became breathless, rough with my instrument, myself.

At the back of the garden was an odd concrete structure that had possibly been built as a room to go alongside a pool, which had never materialised. It had long glass windows along one side, so Billy decided to use it as his studio. Beyond it was a small grouping of juniper trees. When I first got there, his materials, works, were stacked neatly against the walls, but as the weeks advanced, the place became wilder and spilled out of itself.

There was a room at the back of the house, on the second floor, which was long and narrow, with a slim window at the end, looking out across the garden, the land dropping away behind it to the valley where the plane and his father had fallen. I placed a chair a metre from the window, so I could see Billy's studio. This was where I played my cello.

I went to the window when I began to panic, quitting my instrument. Because of the trees around the garden, the junipers and some pines, the sunlight came blazing onto it in columns, and within these columns, other things could be seen, illuminated: pollen, insects. In his studio, Billy was often sitting in the light by the windows sketching on a pad of paper, and the movements of his arm alternated between fast and slow, but always they seemed to betray a dogged sense of fury.

I asked about this; I wanted to know what he spent his days doing. He explained he was sketching his father, from memory, he could not stop trying to get him. Yet everything he tried was lifeless.

*

We fought only a few days after my arrival. I'd suggested we dismantle the pile of his father's belongings from the living room, or at least rescue some of the items, because the house was too empty. I believed I was being practical. We needed some more furniture. But I was also disturbed by the pile, the mania it suggested; I did not think it was a wise idea to live with this, or a room we could not go inside. Billy disagreed and called me insensitive, and he wouldn't let me touch any part of it. That was the fact that worried me—preserving all of it was too peculiar. There were pots and pans I wanted. Also, there was the sense of order—I wanted to know how we would achieve living there, what it might seem like.

I hadn't realised he was sentimental in this way, which is how his attachment to that pile appeared to me, but he became vicious, hostile when I mentioned it.

'It's not sentimental. It's a lack of sentiment. It's a lack of anything.'

'It's scary.'

'So? It's meant to be.'

This was what was new: it was no longer my pain taking precedence. This shocked me, of course, in the way it does when melancholy has become a habit. If I were to say there was something welcome in this, it wouldn't be exactly what I mean, yet it would get somewhere towards the truth. It was an acknowledgement of change. He thought it was terrible, that I could become so suddenly practical, heartless, when for months at home I'd been the opposite.

'I had to wash your hair,' he reminded me.

But I did sense there was a proper way to do things. I wanted to regain my precision.

I decided I'd drive out to the nearest town early each morning to have coffee, then return home whilst it was still early, so that I could play my cello having gained a sense of elsewhere. On the night I decided to do this, I went to sleep confident in my commitment. Yet in that town, the next morning, I wandered.

I had the idea I might like to sit in a square, at a cafe eating slices of ham or pastries, but I could not find the place I pictured. Every situation was off slightly, and I walked past two or three cafes not sitting down, until I'd walked so far that I'd gone back to the first one. When I got there, I realised the coffee didn't really matter and it was getting late, so I drove home without having anything. I did this endlessly. I went off searching for something, and when I found it (a specific cheese, a church I wanted to visit, moisturiser from the pharmacy) I realised I could do without it, or I could do it at another time, and so I would go back to where I came from, emptyhanded, restless.

At lunchtime, I sat on the porch drinking small, red cans of beer, looking out to the road, the same sonatas, concertos, on my headphones. Once I was drunk, I attempted to practise. I played wildly for a few hours, disliking what I heard, and then I would remain with my cello, feeling full in a hollow way from the alcohol. I'd wanted to be a soloist, and I could not escape the fact of how solitary I was there. And how much older I felt than I liked, sitting watching a closed door, willing it to open.

On a Thursday morning, I drove to town again. I wasn't sure what I wanted, except to finally purchase something and hold it in my hands and take it home with me, so I went to the supermarket. I parked in the town square then walked fifteen minutes until I found the small shop. Inside, I bought a cantaloupe melon. Its tail smelt ripe and sweet, a little salty. I was pleased. I held it carefully against my body. But when I started walking back to the car, I wasn't sure in which direction I'd arrived at the supermarket. The hot streets of the town were deserted, shutters pulled across the windows, so I could not find anyone to ask for directions, and I was not able to get a sense of where I was within it. I cradled the melon in my arms and walked continually through these streets, the shuttered windows surrounding me.

The town was a labyrinth, and I had no idea how to get where I needed. I looked at the map on my phone, yet I couldn't find a square anywhere, and I began to think even if I found our car, it might have somehow been transformed, become unrecognisable. For a second, I considered phoning Billy, asking him to help me. Instead, I walked in many different directions, turning constantly, coming again and again to the same places.

By the time I emerged onto the wide street, lined by jacaranda trees, which I recognised, I was desperate. My eyes were hurting from the heat, my heels sore from rubbing against my trainers. A long, thin strip of dusty ground lay in the middle of this street, a garden of sorts, and the houses stood far back from the pavement, which must've been the source of my confusion because it was not a square at all.

A group of old men sat in the middle of this garden on chairs the colour of egg yolk. They sat just in front of our car, so when I walked towards it, they turned in their chairs, smiling to each other. I got in the front seat and put the melon on the passenger side, where it rolled onto the floor. It sat in the dirty foot bed whilst I began crying without covering my face, staring through the windscreen at the group of old men, chatting among themselves, looking at me occasionally.

They ignored me, but it did not feel indifferent. It felt like they were trying to teach me something about minuteness: the time we spend here, the insignificance of a single hour, a single melon.

The problem was this presence of doubt, where before there had never been any. It was like a slim opening had appeared before me, a crack in the wall, just enough to peer out of, and through this I could gain a different perspective—I did not know what perspective because I did not dare peer through the opening, being unsure what I might see, whose perspective I would be gaining, but it was enough that the opening was there, allowing the possible fact of another reality to be known, where alternative light, weather, might be imagined, neither better nor worse, only existing.

The idea of someone else discovering this was my great source of fear. I was in contact with the cellist I'd studied under in Paris, and I sensed she realised something. She was disturbed by what had happened, but more so by my continued reluctance to reveal the extent of my issues. She insisted on hearing updates about the strength of my panic, the comings and goings of fear, anger. She wanted me to play for her over video call, perhaps to prove my talent was not so easily arrested. It was a talent she had nurtured, and she felt a claim to it, yet I could not do this. I would not play for her at all. That disturbed her further. She asked both why I was not properly alarmed about what was happening, and why I wasn't able to get over it, but I did not know how to correctly display alarm, and I did not know what I needed to get over.

Nothing had happened, apart from my playing had grown awful. I'd lost all my ability, and I did not want her to hear this. It was excruciating, unthinkable to reveal.

Alone in my upstairs room, I tried again to practise my way out of panic. I retreated, desperately, to Bach. I began playing his Suite No. 5 in C-Minor, tuning my A-string down to G, focusing on the Sarabande. I stopped and started, checking the annotations I'd made on the manuscript, experimenting with the tempo. It did not sound good. It was as if I could no longer discover the true notes, the series of actions required to reach them. My wrist and the muscles in my back were stiff, the music without resonance. It became hotter and I went to the window, turned back, sat down again, sweating. It was Anna Magdalena's manuscript that I used—Bach's wife. She was a singer. She'd copied out all his scripts for him.

Billy's voice arrived, faintly, in the room through the open window.

'Luc?'

I put down my cello, and I went to my vantage point. He was standing in the middle of the garden, squinting up to the left of where I stood. It must still have been early, as the sun was in the east, ahead of him. The air smelt of the juniper trees, the heat already rousing itself. It was possible he couldn't see my position, as the sun shone directly on his face. We hadn't really spoken for days, it seemed, and yet I knew what he'd been doing. When I wasn't practising, I watched him in his studio from my window. He was always in his studio.

'What was that?' he said.

'Bach.'

'It was sad.'

'I know.'

'It was lonely. What was that?'

'Bach. It was bad, sorry, I forgot you could hear.'

'I said it was *sad*, suddenly really sad.'

'Yes, there's no chords. I get it.'

'Why are there no chords?'

I frowned down on him.

'The harmony is only implied.' I shouted, much louder than necessary. 'It's supposed to be beautiful.'

A lot of the time, I returned to the image of someone standing in the audience. Past the lights, someone, standing when they shouldn't, my cello tossed on the floor, the knowledge, privately, of dying. I returned to that image, also, when I looked down on him from that window. Except I hadn't been able to see the face of the person in the audience, and I could see Billy's face clearly in the garden. It was him who could not see me, with the sun in his eyes.

Billy's first solo show with the gallery was arranged for spring. This was the show that would change things for him, but, of course, he did not know that yet. He was nervous. I had a sense of it. He had spoken to me about what he'd been working on, how it was to be many different pieces that would be arranged together, each a different iteration of the others. But there would be no perfect form to begin from, no archetype. They were to be very tall and thin. What was it about? He told me *fragility*, which was not at all the answer I'd expected. *Imposter* had been the word in my mind. It had been the word in my mind ever since he'd first described that house to me.

Often, I went to the slim window in my room upstairs. When Billy came to the front of his studio, I watched him from this position. He was always shirtless, hair sweaty, body bent over objects or pieces of paper, hands involved in many processes. I presumed he was still trying to draw his father, but there seemed to be other tasks too, involving equipment I couldn't identify, which he spent hours on, his head bent, serious. He worked relentlessly. Every time I looked there seemed to be some new action, the contents of the studio mushrooming, forms and materials growing on the floor and tables. He never noticed me watching, my face at the glass. I never told him I was watching.

He had spoken of lifelessness, but he was creating, madly. The lifelessness must not have taken root, I thought. Or else, it was not his own lifelessness he'd encountered.

I was not always sure where we'd arrived at as a couple. Where the house had come from. What we expected of ourselves.

One weekend, I woke late and hungry to find nothing in the fridge but half an onion and some milk that I could not remember buying but drank the entirety of, so I drove to a tiny village nearby where there was a grocer's. I intended to buy vegetables. It was hazy, which I'd been told was unusual at that time in the year. The silvery road came in and out of focus. In the village, there were few people.

The shop was nearly empty, and I began putting leafy, bitter-looking greens, small potatoes, into my basket, picking at berries, smelling the peaches and wondering what I could buy for Billy, to please him, which wouldn't be expensive. We were only living on the money left with the house, and whatever teaching I was able to do over video call. Occasionally I'd hear the grocer exchange a few words with someone passing the entrance.

At one point, I turned around, holding a bulb of fennel, and saw the grocer wrapping a large amount of beautiful, red grapes—really, almost a deep brown—in many sheets of white paper. The colour of the fruit was so magnificent it seemed ancient, and I thought I must never have tasted grapes that were that ripe looking, succulent. The grocer appeared to be taking extreme care over their packaging. A tall man stood next to him, and I had the sense, as I looked toward his face, that he might be familiar. So, I was surprised to realise it was Billy. I opened my mouth to say something before his expression stopped me. He was staring intently in front of him, but there was a blankness to his eyes, which gave me the idea he might not know me.

He was wearing a long, grey trench coat that I did not recognise, almost worn through at the elbows. It was completely wrong for the weather. His hands clutched the front of the coat to him, so much that he was white knuckled. The lines of his face seemed harder, and his broad cheekbones more prominent. On top of them were patches of fuchsia.

He appeared so unlike himself. When the grocer spoke to him, Billy did not look him in the eye, but gave him the money as if it were something clandestine that they were involved in, and then he put four large oranges, which were on the table, into his coat's deep pockets, taking the package of grapes quickly, holding them to his chest beneath the trench coat. The manner in which he did this, the care and focus of his body, how closely he held the package to his skin, stirred something in mine, and it seemed sexual, the way he was holding those fruits to himself. Why was he doing that? I was shocked at the prospect of his blank eyes, the idea of them turning to me yet not changing whilst he held the fruits so intimately. I was outraged, too, about this other face he wore, without my knowledge.

The grocer had a handful of change to give him, but Billy seemed unable to loosen his grip on the package of grapes, so the grocer put each coin carefully into his pockets, with the oranges. Gold cents and oranges together, I thought. Behind his head there was a mirror, and I caught sight of myself.

Where my eyes were, I saw only shadows, and they had the dark of old pennies, as if they'd been lain over my eyes as gently as the grocer had placed the coins one by one in Billy's pockets. Pennies on my face.

I said his name. I said his name out loud to stop the insistent trooping of these images, but he had gone, he had his back turned, he did not hear, he was leaving. I was too late.

I did not mention that incident to him, at any point. On one level, this was because I knew I wouldn't be able to capture the strangeness for him, after the fact, and on another level, it was because I knew he'd seen me. I knew the strangeness could only have come about from a sense of recognition, a joint enterprise, which somehow did not lead anywhere, did not translate in the usual way to acknowledgement or communication. Something had blocked it, and I sensed this thing was to do with how we were in love. I can't say why this is true. I can't put it to words. I know it is true despite the words I can't find to explain it. It kept us away from each other. It was disruptive.

After that I waited until the next time he left on his bike, then went down to his studio. It was cluttered in there in a way that suggested familiarity—I could see the paths of his hands across the tables. It was different to how his studio had been at home, and the difference suggested a change that must also have been internal—new ways of conceiving, of relating to his work.

I was looking for his old sketches. The walls of the house were bare since Billy had stripped them, and I'd imagined putting up some of his drawings, so we might have something to look at in the evenings when we ate dinner. After that sighting of him in the grocer's, I was also snooping. I felt we were together and yet we were not so. I couldn't discover the truth of this nature: we barely spoke over dinner but drank and caressed each other, had sex but only after listening to music loud enough that I felt it hid some silence, some withdrawal. In the hottest part of the night, I left our bed to lie with my cello, where I could feel the air through the open window, and where my body felt like something else: half-formed, hazardous, yet cleaner somehow. Continuous.

The juniper trees around the studio meant the sunlight entered that space in queer shapes and figures, and these were among the shapes and figures of his sculptures, so the place was a tapestry of forms. It took me a while to find his old sketchpads at the back, all the same type and make, which I recognised, and when I went through the pile, flipping the pages, stopping and starting, I found a lot of sketches of his own face from years earlier, before we were together, which seemed miraculous, in the way they appeared among the pages, like a lost person returning—a stranger from him.

There was a sketchpad that was more damaged than the rest. It contained the studies of me he'd made for the sculpture, and also others, which I couldn't remember him making. I knew they were of me because he'd named and dated them, but without the words, I probably wouldn't have recognised myself. They included detailed studies of my joints, the connections between different parts of my torso. I looked at those points on my body in the studio. I looked back at the sketches, inspected my figure again, found it seemed wrong. I did this for some time. I did it for so long I forgot why I'd come there.

A branch touched the roof. The heat seemed to rise with a gust through the open door. I had an overwhelming sense of hostility. Suddenly, the studio did not feel like the space of someone I knew. I realised, I was afraid of being there, frightened of the fact of my solitude. It seemed to me I'd never been afraid to be alone before him.

His sculptures loomed, elegantly, in the welts of sunlight. I had been preoccupied with loss since I'd been with him, and it occurred to me this loss might be the shadow of one already experienced, a loss I could not give a name to, which had happened when I'd met him, when we'd fallen in love with each other. And so, loss—he taught me loss, too, long before I ever lost him.

I left the studio because of how it was affecting me. It was the afternoon, and the heat was intolerable. Even inside, with air conditioning, where it should've been cooler, I found myself overheating, my pulse beginning to beat hard and loudly in my ears. I couldn't breathe, it seemed, in that country.

He arrived home and beamed to find me in the garden with one of his sketches, which I'd forgotten I was holding. He told me he'd bought some fruits and cheese from the nearest market. He described the food in detail, and it was as if he was describing me, in the same way he'd taken the parts of my body and detailed them, fixing them to his pages. I saw how easy he was with my presence, how it didn't startle him to know I'd been in his studio, and I grew enraged by his calmness. I resented how he could fling out his love as he wanted, as if it didn't change him.

On the first day there, he'd told me as soon as I became unhappy, I could go home, and that it wouldn't matter. In my head, I queried the truth of those two sentences as he stood there talking about dinner. I knew we would eat once more in silence, touching each other, covetous. I wasn't happy. This was true even though being with him, happiness seemed, as an object, so much realer.

Was this love, also, this wall I came up against?

Whilst we were staying at the house, an artist Billy admired was staying with his wife in Seville. They were staying in a well put together flat in an artistic area of the city, with their small dog, and they were famous within the art world although they were not famous in a wider sense. The man was in his sixties. He'd been working for forty years. All this I knew from Billy. He was fixated by this man's work, and so when his gallery arranged for a meeting between them, he was more agitated than I'd ever seen him. He was pacing about the garden drinking water. It was suggested all four of us could have dinner, he told me, and I couldn't work out who else he was including.

'His wife and you,' Billy said.

I did not want to meet these people. The names he had for them, even, seemed fearful. The artist, his wife. I grew anxious as to how we would introduce ourselves, what had Billy already told this man, what title might I be awarded? But he was so excited. I told myself not to linger here, in this place of insecurity.

First, we were to meet at a tapas bar, then numerous different restaurants. They moved between formal and casual, lunch and dinner. Finally, they decided that in the morning they would go to the market in Triana to buy some fish, and they'd cook lunch for us in their flat, where we could spend the afternoon. They wanted to offer us this, they said. They were clear on that point—that they would be offering something. I did not know what they planned to offer.

Billy drove, so I would drive back. The flat was in Feria, on a road called *Los Inocentes*, which was cool and narrow, where young men or women walked with rucksacks or buggies. It was in a tall, stone building with a central courtyard. The artist and his wife met us at the top of the stairs with the little black dog that rubbed against our ankles. Their flat had access to a roof terrace, which they took us up to, shutting the dog behind a door, at which it whined, mournfully. From the roof, all the other roofs of Seville were visible, even to some extent, accessible, and it was as if we had travelled to another world of sky and laundry lines, clean linen rising in the breeze, the figures of men smoking, leaning over the parapets. The steeples of many churches rose around us, and when the bells rang, which they did quite often, it was deafening.

'What a sound,' I said, and the woman looked at me.

'The man who owns the apartment thought we might mind. Really, I think it's thrilling, as if something is coming.'

She spoke with a French accent. She was from Marseille, she told us. She was wearing a green waistcoat, a long skirt, silver bracelets. Various parts of her caught the light—buttons, earrings. He was in a crumpled shirt, black cotton trousers.

'In Marseille all the buildings begin to crumble,' she said. 'And no one gives a shit because the rich want to rebuild.'

She smiled at me with her lips closed after every sentence, which made me wary. She was forward, friendly, in a way that suggested practise. The sky was completely blue. The man asked Billy about our circumstances, and I listened to him detail his father's death, the challenge of living there, the sense of not knowing what to do with the contents of the house. He told them he felt he was waiting for his father to return and sort things out. He had explained this to me before, but this time what he said was slightly altered. Before he hadn't spoken of waiting—I thought he'd spoken of fearing, although I couldn't remember exactly, and the difference, my inability to recall, made everything feel unfocused. I was struck suddenly to be sitting in the sun opposite strangers.

'And Luciana's been—' he paused, gesturing to me, unsure, willing me to intervene. 'Working,' he finished.

'What have you been working on?' the artist said. His eyes were almost white, but filmy, gentle.

'I don't know.'

I stared at Billy, who was also staring back, blankly, without assistance. He had never used my full name before, which I only used professionally, for performance. I couldn't work out why he had just then.

'I had a failure,' I said. 'Something disturbed me.'

'Oh, well…' the artist said, refilling my wine glass.

'A big failing?'

The woman touched her neck, leant closer. I didn't like the gesture. It was another that seemed practised, a signal of her womanhood, reminding me of who she was, who I was, and to whom I should be confiding: the tacitly agreed structures of the meeting.

'Failure is necessary, no?' she said, this time even softer.

'I don't really care if it is.'

'Luc's classically trained,' Billy said, 'she's been performing since she was six.'

All three of them laughed, and Billy put his hand on the back of my chair. Again, I had never heard him talk in that way: turn me out to ease a situation. I did not see what was funny. The woman was a poet, she said.

'I fail most of the day, most of each hour, sometimes. It's the only way I know to change.'

Her last sentence seemed odd, possibly mistranslated, but I didn't feel I could ask her to explain further, having been so reticent. Possibly I didn't want to hear this woman be articulate in a way I couldn't be. They were being kind, I realised, but I didn't want to speak about these things with strangers. Their togetherness was tidy. I wondered if their art felt the same way. I wondered if they were happy when they woke and when they went to bed, if they said cruel things to each other, how cruel those things might become. I would've liked to hear a bad word spoken between them, or to know if they always still remembered to say things, good or bad, to each other. But, also, I liked to hear how her silver bangles came together as she put her arm gently on her husband's leg. Billy shifted, continually, his arm tilting my chair a little, his nervousness creating the appearance of someone arrogant.

We ate fish for lunch, down in the large kitchen, and the conversation turned to the artist's work. He spoke for a long time about the environment, senses of destruction, waste. He was animated when he spoke about methane escaping from the seabed; the film left his eyes and their whiteness seemed more persecutory. He became unaware, too, of his wife, who was checking a dish in the oven. He spoke about doing things, and I wondered what it was he thought he could do, what he was trying to tell us.

The fish was delicious. The woman, the poet, had cooked it whole on a bed of lemons with white onions. I could see the golden skin of the onions all over the counters in the kitchen. She told me about the recipe, how she'd selected the fish, how to look in their eyes and see how recent their death. A shiver ran through me as she explained this. I had the urge to ask her to tell me further things, but the urge was irritating. I could not think of anything further to ask her.

All the time she was talking so was her husband, still, about the environment. Eventually, the conversation moved to Billy's work, as we pulled bones out of the white flesh. He spoke about the various materials he was working with, how it was important that fragility was maintained in the work, about a need to do away with romance in order to focus on labour, so that nothing was done seamlessly, and the effort undertaken was always evident.

'And what will you call it?' the artist said.

He had not mentioned a title to me, so I assumed he had not come up with one. But he said,

'Fugue.'

And he seemed quite certain. I'd never heard him say that word. My surprise was uncomfortable, in front of these people.

'A fugue state?' the poet replied.

This was something else I hadn't heard, knowing only about the word through music.

'What's that?' I asked. And the simplicity of the question seemed at odds with the elegance of their conversation. Although he looked at me, Billy did not seem to hear what I'd said, instead speaking of something different.

'When I came here,' he explained, 'I thought I'd get some closure. I thought being in the house would let me take on a role that I'd always felt I should reject. I could be a son and that would allow me to see my father better, in context, so his abandonment would only be a part of who he was, one part of many things, and the other things could tell me something about him, like why he did it.'

He drank a little from his wine glass.

'Instead, I feel like an imposter. I can't take on the role. I don't understand him any better. At the same time, I don't feel how I used to, before I came here, so I'm stuck between two variants of myself. My image seems to multiply, and it becomes more fragile. Sometimes this feels suffocating, at other times freeing. I don't know what I'm more frightened of. I don't know if I should go back or forward.'

I'd heard bits and pieces of what he was speaking about before, told to me often in liminal moments, as we were dressing, just before we fell asleep, although I hadn't heard all of these thoughts put together as one, so that they moved from one to another neatly and became artful. The refinement seemed to take away something. I was no longer sure of what he meant. I wondered when it was that he'd begun framing himself in this way, and why I hadn't noticed. I wondered if it was only for the artist's benefit, if I was only witnessing a performance. If so, I didn't like it, didn't know him. It seemed to go against what he'd said earlier—there was no sense of how hard it must have been to articulate in the first place. It felt too practised.

I noticed that, unlike me, the artist and the poet seemed pleased with what he'd said, smiling slightly, nodding, and this was annoying, because what he'd said was not pleasing. The contents of what he'd said were distressing, even though the way he'd expressed himself was elegant. Billy seemed tired, and I wanted to hold him, but it wasn't feasible. Really, I wanted to tell him we could go, we did not need to keep this up, to entertain these people.

'I'm always struck by a desire, both to stay and to go,' the poet said, interrupting what I had felt as a private train of thought between Billy and me. 'To look harder and to turn away, is how it feels. That state, the one and the other, both at the same time. Maybe it's better to do one thing rather than the other, to get into the world. But to do that might require a boldness, to be willing to get dirty, which I'm not sure I have an interest in.'

'Why not?' he replied.

'I'm not sure. Maybe I'd be a better poet, but I'd be kidding myself, no? Fooling myself, is how it feels.'

There was silence around the table, when all the words just spoken seemed to settle, and I grew depressed in the silence. I wasn't sure what the poet meant, if she meant anything. I looked about the kitchen, noticing a short list of items on the door of the fridge. The words were French: *veau, glace, roses de chou,* presented like pretty children. I glanced, without thinking, towards the artist, after taking this in, who was staring at me. He winked. It was a short, sharp, movement, so at odds with the mood of the room it seemed outrageous. Perhaps, he thought I was bored, or perhaps he was attempting to form some private intimacy between us, in the way that the conversation between his wife and Billy had seemed in some ways private. It was flippant, and I could sense him smiling after I looked away, down to the green leaf-like pattern on the dishes.

'And how are you going to get more disciplined, to get where you want to be?'

I looked up, and he was still staring at me.

'You seem unsure, I think?' he added. 'When you have a failure, you need to keep going.'

'You make things too simple,' the poet said, smiling at me, batting her husband.

I turned to Billy, who did not say anything. I did feel, abruptly, at a distance from him. I looked back to the neat list on the fridge, repeating the three words in my head dumbly, because I could not translate them.

'My discipline was difficult for our relationship,' I said.

'But life is compromise,' the artist replied, and I nearly rolled my eyes.

He was still staring at me, but this time there was no winking; rather his chin was lifted, making him look faintly hostile. Perhaps he'd seen my disdain anyway. I suspected, then, I would be treated with more apprehension at that table, having twice been unable to account for myself. Yet something strange happened. The moment passed. I was not rejected.

It was only slowly, after they alluded to our life a few times, what our future might look like, if we would stay there, if we would return, if I ever helped Billy with his work, that I realised I was already accounted for. I was his partner. I did not need to present any other case for myself. This, the safety of this, the unwillingness to look clearly at things, to see who I was, how difficult I was being, was intolerable as soon as I realised it. I excused myself to use their bathroom. Inside, I opened the window over the toilet, put my face to the opening for a moment, until I regained a level of calmness.

Their belongings, half spilling out of two wash bags, were placed around the sink. There was a clear, green bottle of perfume next to hers, which smelt of cypress trees. A few more pieces of heavy silver jewellery lay around, and I imagined what it might feel like to be this woman: to put each piece on in the morning and then in the evening take them off—if their solidness conveyed itself to her, so she felt solid for owning them.

I went to the sink and opened the cabinet, the drawers, rifled through what I found there—floss, tampons, pills of various kinds. I touched each object I found, even her diaphragm, and in doing this became satisfied that these people were like us also, that their lives could be banal, inescapable. When I went back, I slid into place, next to Billy. The dirty plates had disappeared to be replaced with bowls in the shape of sunflowers, and I found myself smiling. There was a tart and sweet wine, fruits, cream. Outside the buzz of the city rose, the bells rang, people wandered. Some people, different people, might have overturned that table, in the artful room, with the artful people.

'And what disturbed you?' the poet asked, once we'd started eating.

'Disturbed?' I repeated.

'You said, something disturbed you, which was why you had your failure.'

I had forgotten that was the way I'd explained myself. For some reason, in front of this woman, I felt unable to explain what had happened in the usual ways. I could not call on panic, anxiety, because I realised what she was telling me, which was that they were only consequences. She wanted to know what made them. This seemed too far, too intimate. Perhaps, for her, words had become things to hide behind, but I did not know how to wield them.

'I wasn't feeling myself.'

'Why?'

She wasn't eating, nor was her voice as soft as it had been. I realised what I had taken for a false intimacy, a desire to get to know me because I was the other woman, was in fact a desire to know this. It seemed obvious at that point she might have known already what had happened, and it seemed obvious she had her own reasons for inquiring, about which I knew nothing. I was repelled by this sense of her mind, her motivations, coming into view beyond the lunch table. The probing felt obscuring: she was requesting an exposure that felt fatal. I did not have a story to offer.

'Why do you care so much?'

My voice was strained, and Billy grabbed my leg beneath the table. Him grabbing my leg like that, so quickly, suggested this moment might've been something he'd anticipated, worried over. I could not recognise myself, or him, in that worry.

The poet laughed although her eyes remained penetrating. She hadn't expected the question, but she could contain it.

'It just seems remarkable, really, to contemplate this moment.'

'And why are you together?' I said.

Then for the first time, she was quiet. To calm down, I pictured all the belongings of their bathroom, kept together, neatly packed and unpacked, all the bodily functions these belongings tended to, the mess of them. The poet and her husband stared at me, either not wanting to answer, or not knowing how.

'How did you meet?' I added.

'Oh.' Her face changed, after a moment, went back to how it had been. 'We were dancing. We both love Slovakian folk music, and we were at a festival. We ended up dancing together.'

The artist went across the room to find his phone, and after spending some time connecting it to a portable black speaker, he played some music, which I assumed was Slovakian folk music, from the way they looked at each other, then at us, both of them pushing their chairs beneath the table, beginning to sing the words of this song, a language I did not know. It was a love song, they told us. They moved suddenly about the room in deft manners, clapping their hands, the poet lifting her skirt to display silky, lean ankles. I was surprised at the beauty of these ankles. She wore sandals with kitten heels, velvet, the colour of liver. She flicked her heels behind her. She was no longer alarmed, no longer concerned with failure. It was folk music, they explained. Did we like it?

Their limbs struck out into space, their faces set now, focused. They had claimed they wanted to offer us something, so it occurred to me this might be the offering. We were there to watch them. Look, they kept saying, you put your foot out like this, your wrists, your hips, you hold your partner's hand, you move in relation to each other's bodies, all over the floor, sometimes gently, sometimes with mettle. The moves do not change, but they might seem more testing, some days. You might want to sit against the wall, forget the dance, close your eyes, forget about the relentlessness. But, they cried, it would be a pity!

The music hastened. The poet's skirt swayed, the artist's bare feet slipped across the tiles, their voices grew breathless. They slapped their knees. Billy and I sat completely still, watching, the remnants of the meal laid out like specimens on the table. The way the afternoon, the poet and the artist, had been subsumed to this dance, was astonishing. It was as if they'd been doing it the entire time without us noticing.

I looked to Billy and was startled to find him looking exactly the same as me, his eyes fixed on the couple, the patterns they were making. I willed him to look at me, willed him now to turn and say we were leaving, as I knew he wanted to. But he didn't. Perhaps he did not want to admit what we were watching. He did not want to admit to falseness, not at where he was, not at the point he was reaching. He just wanted to get through it.

The artist extended his arm,

'But we'll teach you! Come over, come here, there's room.'

Billy got up from his chair, so I grabbed his arm. I didn't want to. I wanted to be out of there, right away, not to stay and do their dance. I wanted to be alone with him, where we could get back to each other. I wanted to go backwards.

'We should go,' I said, beneath the music. 'I can't get up and do that.'

'We'll go once we've danced a little.'

'No. I don't want to dance! I can't do it.'

The poet came over.

'Oh, but you must be bored! You're not drinking—let us call you a cab in a bit, it's no trouble. Stay, have something to drink, we can make Negronis—'

'No. Thank you, anyway. I don't feel well.'

'You feel fine,' he said. 'Stop being like this.'

I couldn't believe he'd say that, in front of these people.

The poet touched him.

'Or you can stay, so Luc can go home, and we'll call you a cab?'

I could not believe he was willing to let me walk out of there alone.

'Yes,' he said. 'I'll do that.'

He didn't understand. How could he not understand? I couldn't do it. Wasn't that for months what I'd been saying?

The artist gave me slices of tart wrapped in tinfoil, and the poet handed me a piece of paper on which she'd written the recipe for the fish. As they did this, their feet still moved to the rhythm of the music, and they touched each other gently. Billy remained in the middle of the room drinking. He did not come towards me. He kept looking at me, and to see him there alone made me feel anguished to be leaving, but I did not want to go to him. I knew what he was doing, knew even he had to do it, but I could not get up and dance with him, even though it felt like a failure, to leave in this way. To leave the dance behind, the sight of him in the afternoon, the room lit the colour of amber, the dying light, his hands reaching out for theirs, the blaring of the music. I did not know what was beyond that. I did not know if there was anything.

Sometimes I seek out photos of him. I set myself limits, so I don't lose my footing in the present, and I try not to read interviews if they accompany the photos, always fearing this life of his made concrete. On the internet there are professional photos of him in his studio, beside his sculptures, blurrier shots of him at events, when he's not aware of the camera. Old friends sometimes post images of him online: at a dinner table tearing some bread, drinking beer on a sofa, waiting to cross a road, turning to look over his shoulder. There is a photo where he is looking at the lens exactly how he used to look at me in the morning.

When I view these images, it is not only him I'm seeing. I see an image of myself, too, as I might've been. I place myself next to him on that road, holding his hand in mine; I imagine the candles of the dinner table casting my face, as well, in their brightness. I see myself beside him, and so I see a self that is all possibility, and she smiles back at me or frowns, speaks or stays silent, is close to him or at a distance. She lives, I know this, I witness her, but I do not know what she's feeling.

Often, I imagine her body lying under him, her feet resting on his bare chest—the soles clammy on his chest, when he places them there. He has placed them there often. Her hips lift, and her mouth is open, moaning possibly, saying nothing, crying nonsense.

Is she happy, I wonder, is she satisfied? Is she a cellist?

To return home was to admit loss in a way I hadn't before, when the endless talk around what had caused my stage fright distracted me from the emptiness of that failure. Then I returned home anyway, and the loss was thorough. In order to do this, I convinced myself it was not as decisive a move as I now view it, and in fact, I believed at one point I would go back. I might even have told him so.

For the first fortnight after my return, we could only text. This was partly due to the patchy signal at the house in Spain, and partly because talking to each other, in complete sentences, was too difficult. He was confused. He did not know what had happened. He maintained I did. At this time, it seemed I was regularly confronted by people who insisted I had an idea of things, a greater comprehension.

Every morning for the first week I sent him a text when I woke. I lay in my parents' spare bed, composing long and short texts that let him know I still existed, that he still existed for me. In some ways, this felt like what I'd been doing the entire time we'd been together. Lying in that hard bed, I was the most aware I've ever been of how badly I loved him—I had a sense of that love physically, in my body, as a living thing with its own consistency, parameters. Yet whenever I sent a text, I also felt I was submitting something for his approval. I wanted to know if I was displaying the correct amount, or type, of emotion. Would it do? Would it convince him? I was not always convinced by the messages that either of us sent. They did not sound honest. Honestly, I'd felt his success as an affliction.

I emailed him. I outlined how little of his attention he'd offered in Spain. I wanted to know why he'd asked me to go with him in the first place. To this he only replied,

So you know how it felt when you were succeeding.

Finally, he phoned, after a fortnight, to say this: he did not know. And after he said it, I didn't either. I didn't know why I'd left, or why we couldn't be together. I explained I had to know—I had to work it out, to see things plainly. He asked me to let it go. To return. But I couldn't do that. I had to be certain. He accused me of stubbornness, of an obsession with control, of never bending.

'How are you always so sure of yourself?' he said.

'But I never am. I'm not sure of anything.'

How could he not see that?

To his mind, I'd abandoned him. I realised this so late after the fact, after booking the flight and calling the cab and leaving, weeks later, lying in that uncomfortable bed, that it stunned me. He hadn't ever voiced this abandonment because he'd considered it obvious, inarguable. But I, too, had felt abandoned. I just hadn't told him.

I could imagine a version of myself that would return. This version was concerned only with the relief he, my love for him, offered: a buoy I was clinging to in deep water. I felt, in some moments, he was enough. He was all I wanted. But in another version of myself, I could not concede, could not simply drift in the deep, could not forgo myself. In fact, in this version, I wanted out of the water.

There must have been other things I never told him. If he believed I was so sure of myself, there must have been other things he didn't realise. There was the sensation of an orchestra playing behind me—had I mentioned that, I wondered, did he see—to be at the centre when the sound becomes movement, and to go somewhere, and possibly to take a crowd, and possibly to have them listen, and for the moment to come and go and to have seen it pass for them too. To have seen it pass over them. I thought I probably hadn't mentioned that, among everything. How much I needed for them to listen.

A month or so after I returned home, I received an email from the composer. We'd spoken little whilst I'd been in Spain, which happened when he was working, so the fruits of his labour had remained far from my mind, held at some distance. This feeling remained as I looked at the empty subject line of the email, noted it contained attachments, understood what he was expecting. I didn't open it. But checking my emails for messages from Billy drew me back there, and for many minutes, whilst I waited for one of Billy's replies, I stared also, without realising, at this email from the composer.

I had resumed teaching, which was the only contact I allowed myself with the cello. I was offered work through people I knew in the industry, mainly with young cellists who were focused and capable, so the lessons were gratifying. My mother had suggested this break, as she was calling it, might be the right time to reconsider my objectives—perhaps, she thought, I might consider taking an academic position, or I could move towards composition. Her hope was I might transition from the stage towards something she viewed as more permanent. She wanted this 'break' to mean a development. It was a notion other people had voiced in different ways—the idea that my failure could lead somewhere.

I had an argument with her whilst I was cooking dinner, which started when I said that if I couldn't perform, I would remain a teacher. I had no interest in academia or composition.

'It's like stagnation,' she replied to this. 'I thought you wanted to do *some*thing.'

'Not something,' I said. 'Not *something*.'

'But there's no solidity in what you've done!'

'I'm supposed to be the solidity.'

She opened her mouth, but for once, she stopped herself. We ate in silence. I knew what she had been about to say, and what could I tell her, now that nothing was working? I could not explain to her the authority of the musician, how it was, for one moment, my interpretation that became the music. I could not tell her how daring this felt, to possess so much, to set the terms of my own performance, because it was no longer what I was doing, and she knew it.

What was in my head, all this time, was the word Billy had used at the artist's dinner table. I'd looked up the origin of that word—*fugue*—later and found it came from the word *flight,* and after this I'd felt myself wanting to describe what had happened to me as a flight. Something that had taken me. This formulation, as deceptive as it was, seemed palatable. The sense of movement, even, felt welcome. I had assumed my mother would see straight through such a deception, but I understood at this point she was also falling prey to it. She too saw my current state as transitory: a strange digression on a course that would eventually be corrected.

The mother of a young girl I was teaching offered me a glass of wine after one of her daughter's lessons. She was the director of programming at one of the major concert halls in London, who had always been supportive, which was why, I assumed, she'd hired me.

We sat together in her large, tiled kitchen, and, after discussing her daughter, she asked how my own playing was, whether Spain had helped me process what had happened. She spoke in a relaxed way, and because she had no personal reasons to enquire but was being friendly, I felt able to speak to her a little. I explained I wasn't sure. I'd given up on the idea of overcoming failure, and instead of expressing dismay or attempting encouragement, she said,

'Yes, I've felt the same way.'

We went on to discuss several young cellists, who were becoming better known and listened to more widely. We agreed they were exciting. I asked, then, after her life, so she spoke about the concert hall and several events she had planned whilst alluding to issues she was having with her husband, who had grown distant to their teenage son for reasons she couldn't unravel. I asked how she had become involved in music events, and she told me, initially, she'd trained as a pianist. She'd studied at a famous conservatoire in Vienna, after which she'd tried, for a few years, to establish a footing back in London.

As she spoke, I noticed a place on her right eyelid where the skin had begun to fold, gently, which could have been a sign of age or could equally have been a shadow cast by the light beside her. Because the effect aged her slightly, I caught a glimpse of this older self, whilst at the same time she spoke of herself younger, and this made our conversation, the fleeting nature of its intimacy, more notable.

I asked why she'd given up the piano.

'Oh,' she said, looking away to her phone on the table. 'I can't think.'

This seemed an odd response, so I waited for her to continue.

'I don't have a reason, exactly, but I suppose I wasn't good enough, though I'm not sure how or why I reached that conclusion.' She shifted in her chair. 'Recently I watched myself back, and really I was better than I remembered, but, anyway, at some point I got over it.'

'What did you get over?'

'The idea of myself.' She took down and then re-clipped her hair with a bright gold pin, in one smooth motion. 'It was part of the performance. It relied on the suspension of disbelief, but I lost that. It stopped mattering.'

From the tone of her voice, I sensed this was true although she seemed to be holding something back.

'You have to dismantle a lot,' she went on. 'I suppose being a failure might be the same as being a success, because you move beyond the thing you were working towards, and I imagine there's some misery in succeeding, because at least with failure the lie that it matters is still there, which I expect, sometimes, it isn't with achievement.'

She smiled, suddenly.

'It was a joy, really, when I decided to give in.'

There was a clarity to her expression that seemed connected to the joy she was describing. The clarity seemed to prove it.

'But you know,' she said, 'I miss hearing you. I was glad when you returned because I thought it might mean something.'

I found myself telling her about the grocer's in Spain, seeing Billy buying those grapes without recognising him, how it was funny. I shouldn't have told her, but I'd wanted to tell someone for a while. It seemed to be the hinge of something—some place between two states—but I couldn't work it out.

'How funny to see someone you love like that!' I said, because it was all I could say.

'But how odd,' she replied. 'And you're no longer together?'

'We're still in love.'

'But how odd, to be in love like that.'

To me, it did not feel odd to be so in love that you hardly know each other. It did feel vast. It did not feel strange.

After I left, I walked back through streets full of fallen leaves to the train station, wondering what might have happened if this woman hadn't got over the idea of herself as a pianist. Perhaps she might have begun to see how her performance, that idea, was singular. She might've realised that everything else in her life contained as much artifice as what she did onstage, but the stage alone was hers. Up there she could be what she decided. That was something. It was a way to live: to know the multitudes of self yet resolve to be one thing, to exist.

What I wondered about though was the joy that had passed briefly across her face when she'd spoke of giving in—why it had seemed so significant.

When I returned to it, the email from the composer was blank. Where the message should've been was white space with only the attachments at the bottom, the scripts that he'd named and numbered. The music was complex, even more so than his previous work, so it took me a few read-throughs to get a handle on what I was facing. There was something solitary about the piece. There were four sections to it, and each part was wildly different in tone, yet there were motifs that were returned to, played upon. The end of the third section was a passage of high, bewildering intensity, which led, as if unendingly, into the next section, containing a fermata, an E flat held longingly.

I could sense such clarity within this note that I became agitated to hear it. I remembered the composer discussing his perfect note, and an E flat had not been what I'd expected, but its arrival in the music seemed to bring something revelatory, as if it were the deep, white eye of a storm. A bracing moment, what the audience sought. The more I read the scripts, the more provoked I felt by this note. But I dreaded the rest of the composition. It contained several prolonged rests, and it was these silences that seemed especially terrifying. They were something I would have to play, just as I played the music. But I didn't want to play silence—silence was what I'd fallen into the last time I was on the stage, and I couldn't face entering it again.

I went to my cello to try the note. The bars preceding it were challenging, and I had not warmed up or prepared myself, so, of course, I struggled. The fingerings were intricate, as were the bow strokes because the script contained no slurs to connect the notes on one bow, making the playing technical, and, in that moment, I lacked all patience, intent only on hearing that one note. I could play it, but without the preceding section there was no clarity. In my head I heard it, and I tried again for a long time, growing tighter, more frustrated, eventually infuriated. I put my cello down roughly and there was the desire to harm something. I stood over its body, imagining my foot through its belly, the strings ripped off, the neck broken.

Over the next few days, the note plagued me. I read the music repeatedly. Each time I did, I seemed to understand more about the nature of its composition, what it was attempting to embody, how my own body might express it, from where each bar might be played. I began carefully on some of the easier sections although in this I was dissatisfied—my playing remained unwieldy.

I went to the composer to speak with him. Even though I couldn't yet play the thing, I wanted to know if I was right, if what I heard was in line with his intentions. I wanted to know if something had been communicated correctly, but he found these questions curious. He told me he did not know yet. He wouldn't know until I'd begun my interpretation.

It was cold in his flat, and I feared at any moment he might ask me to go. When he didn't, I told him about Spain, about leaving. Being with him, I did not feel the same need to prove my love for Billy, so what I said was different to what I'd said to other people, more resigned, and in this there was some respite. I could tell him the extent to which I found it all exhausting.

After I'd finished talking it seemed easier to stay, and he offered me dinner, and we spoke some more about his composition. But when I went home, I became ashamed of having spoken that way to him, as if love was nothing, when I still lived in its presence.

Billy and I were, at that point, only talking late at night. The dark silence of the exterior world made it feel like we were less obliged to say things that were reasonable. We spoke without the wider contexts of our lives seeming relevant. I did not talk about visiting the composer. He did not mention his exhibition. We spoke of private thoughts that might not have existed if it weren't for the other being there to hear them. Yet these conversations, as intimate as they were, did not resolve anything. He was in Spain, and I was in London.

Then he emailed to say that he was returning, and he wanted to see me. He was coming back for two days only, to update his gallery on the progress he'd made. He couldn't stay longer, he explained. He wished he could, but he had to get back to his work. He did not trust himself to be parted from it too long, in case he snapped the thread by which he'd tied himself. He had a lunchtime free, which was when he thought we might meet. Why did he only have a lunchtime? This was immediately my concern. Was it to guard himself against possible rejection, or was it to guard himself against me, not to let me back in so easily?

I replied, a day later, agreeing to lunch in a pub he'd suggested, in Clerkenwell. After sending the email, I read back through all our other conversations, and doing this it seemed, sometimes, that our issues were not all unsolvable. Rather, they seemed to spread between us in an arrangement which I simply could not gather the significance of. Really, they were spread out like standing stones, mysterious, unmoveable markers of our time together. Perhaps, I thought, the confusion was just about how a life together should look—if all this difficulty was to be expected.

I spent the week before our meeting in an excessive mood of anticipation. I believed speaking in person would help us gain lucidity, an understanding of how to free ourselves from the situation. This meeting, I became certain, would bring a change—though I didn't know what change would look like. Unable to bear the silence of the day, I began to practise the composer's music in earnest. I played in my parents' spare room, where the carpet made the acoustics unforgiving, and the fact of how dead the sound was made the stage seem even more distant. It was the first time in years I'd played my instrument without thought of an eventual performance. This made it difficult to do. It did not make it easier. The music felt boundless, and I was now untethered.

It was endlessly wrong, but when that note came it was like a bright vein of insistence, the thing to play for, and I kept going. It drew me forwards. I felt that if I could only hear it aloud as I had in my head, I might find the relief, the profound reprieve, it seemed to offer. I was absorbed by this music, and yet, it wasn't what I wanted. As he got closer, Billy was what I wanted.

On the day we were supposed to meet I woke early. It was the beginning of December and dawn did not emerge until late in the morning. The sky remained silver, barely illuminated. I thought of the heat in Spain, the sense of the country's enormity. I remembered how hard it had been to breathe there, and I was glad I would be seeing Billy back in the city we both knew, where we were known to each other.

I practised the composer's music all day until an hour before we were supposed to meet. The sky remained overcast, and I found myself disoriented about what time it was. I checked my phone continually. Then, as I was winding up, sitting silently in the room with my cello, Billy called. Seeing his name on the screen left me nauseous. I suspected he might be cancelling, and I didn't know how to take this. I answered reluctantly.

'Where are you?' he said. His voice was upset, unexpected.

'I'm at home.'

'Why aren't you here?'

'It's not time yet. It's not three.'

'We weren't meeting at three, three is when I had to leave.'

I said it was impossible. I wrote down the time. I was certain. He asked how long it would take me to get there, and when I said forty-five minutes, he just said,

'Luc, I have to be somewhere.'

I could hear traffic in the background and hearing his voice among the sounds of the city made his return suddenly real.

'Where do you have to be?'

'At the gallery.'

'And after that?'

'We're going to dinner.'

'Could I come after dinner?'

He paused, and I tried to imagine how his face looked, if he was hurt, if he was angry.

'I'll be out. I don't know when I'll finish, and my flight's early.'

There was a terrible silence. After a moment he said, impotently,

'This was when we were meeting.'

What he sounded most was startled. I asked when he'd be back again. He said in a while, he'd let me know. Because I began crying, he told me it would be alright.

'But I want to see you,' I said. 'I've been so wanting to see you.'

After he hung up, I wondered if I was the one that was angry. It seemed so long since I'd known what I was feeling. I imagined what it would take to get to him. Could I go to his gallery? Would he be annoyed if I interrupted? Would he hold it against me? I imagined putting on my coat, navigating my way through the city's streets, dim from the clouds and the season, arriving at his gallery just as he did, just as the sun, which all day had been useless, was setting. I pictured the glow of the gallery's lights illuminating me, red-faced, not knowing what to say. But present. There with him. Perhaps that was all that was necessary.

Yet, I didn't stand up. I sat with my cello imagining this scenario for so long that the time for action was over. The impression of something leaving me was strong—a physical sense of slippage.

Loss in itself was not novel, because there'd always been loss—there had always been distance between him and I, never only closeness. But there was something different this time. What was it that made this loss, this distance, feel so definitive?

There was a morning early on in our relationship when he slipped on the stairs in my old flat. I was in the kitchen as his heel went on the worn carpet, and he flew to the landing below making no noise except for the thud of his body against the banisters. I came running from the kitchen to find him squatting on the carpet, dazed, laughing. He informed me I'd almost lost him. And it was funny, the suddenness of the disturbance, his lack of composure. I laughed with him—he was not hurt—but I remember the apprehension of pain in his voice, the sight of him on the landing, his eyes shining with the small rush of adrenaline, the sense of the fall between us.

After we did not see each other that December, I began to grow nauseous in the afternoons. In the mornings I could act normally, but after midday everything felt inconsequential, like I'd done it a thousand times, and I became sick of myself. Outside of my teaching, I did not see anyone but the composer, and I did not do much but play his music. It was the only thing that felt new. The music, the way in which it danced with the silence it emerged from, anticipating, disrupting, gave substance to a period of nothingness. In which the loss of Billy was a grief I did not believe I'd overcome. The silence was, similarly, the burden of that music.

The composer had begun dating a man he'd met on the night bus, and when the time came to record his music in early spring, when the cold was less persistent, he punctuated our progress in the studio with updates on this romance. His stories often took on a sense of the confessional, because of the hushed, muffling effect of that space. He took me through his doubts, his excitement and frustrations. Our progress on the record was slow and often disheartening, but I was compelled to come in every day by the undulation of these stories, the way in which things were at some points hostile, then ruined, and then, of course, repaired, joyful again. I wanted to know what would happen: where they'd end up, if they'd make it.

One day he told me they'd been on a trip to the Horniman museum, where they'd been allowed to touch the beautiful exhibits, including puppets, which were eerie, fantastical, and wooden masks through which they'd stared at each other. These objects, passed between them, became more fascinating, but he was scared to imagine how many others had touched them, and to think where those people were at that moment.

'It was like a sort of vertigo,' he said, 'how quickly the stuff came and went. I couldn't stop thinking about how easily objects become bizarre and useless. And then, the masks changed him. It was horrible.'

He admitted he'd been disturbed the last few nights because he had no control over what was coming with this man. This was a new experience. Usually, his fears could be placated by moving further inside his work, so that he became numb to everything other than what he was creating. But, he said, the future, seen through the prism of this man and sex and loving him, felt anarchic.

He looked at me,

'But you know what I mean.'

'I do?'

I wasn't sure that I did.

'In that house, in Spain, was all chaos,' he said, with some surprise. 'And you put yourself back in order.'

Just before Billy's show opened, I texted him to say good luck. We'd had a conversation about whether or not I should come to the private view but decided it would be too distressing. He had not been in London much, and so we still hadn't seen each other. To see him among so many people in that gallery would be, I felt, to see him as a stranger—the artist—and I didn't know what role that would grant me. Was this what the composer meant, about order?

I texted Billy again on the opening day to tell him how proud I was of him, and he sent back a reply that said *thank you* just like that, without even a capital letter. I imagined he must've been busy, too stressed to connect with my feelings, which anyway were only being delivered over text. It wasn't until a few days later that I wondered if he'd met someone. It seemed unlikely, he'd been in Spain where, presumably, he hadn't been socialising much, but I remembered the lunch we'd had in Seville, the way the poet had engaged with him. Women engaged with him like that, often quickly.

I explained this all to the composer in the studio who said, of course, it was possible. He asked if it made me think differently about our separation, but it wasn't clear how it should make me feel differently. I was already against the separation. I just couldn't discover a route back.

Billy's show got some attention. I saw his photo on a news website, which I was not expecting—it felt incredible, really unbelievable to see him there. I read the review a few times, and it was as if there was no distance between us, but when I emailed him again, saying this, about how glad I was for him, he sent me back another short message with little or no punctuation, expressing his thanks, telling me that when he had more time he wanted to speak properly.

Then the distance appeared again. I was behind him. It felt like things were more conclusively over because he was experiencing all this without me. At this point, I became sick with a flu that left me feverish and unable to digest anything but lemonade. A week or so later, after we resumed, the recording with the composer became easier. Then it was completed.

The music had diminished at the same time it had strengthened. What had come out of our practice was a stubborn sense of lack, and it was this lack—what was left behind the note, what the note made so apparent—that became the truth of the composition. The sound, paradoxically, was how the lack was articulated. The notes became sparser even in the moments of great intensity; there was a stretching out of what was bearable. It was about the clearing away of circumstance, the ascendence of the feeling, the composer said. In this, my playing returned. It did not return to how it had been, but I was able to play this music. I found my interpretation, and I was able to play this better than anyone else would've.

Eight months after I returned home, I returned to the stage. When I walked out, the rest of the space was so dark it was as if it wasn't there at all. I felt as if I was walking into a box, the walls of which were not visible, and the further I walked, the smaller the box became, until it was just the size of the space taken up by my chair, my instrument. I'd agreed with the composer that if I panicked, I would simply stop playing. I would take the time to regain myself.

We had rehearsed like this, so I knew in some ways it was part of the performance. The nature of the music allowed for it. In many ways, he'd like for it to happen. What I wanted, though, was not to panic, was to go right to the heart of the thing, to play without thought.

I passed into this space without consequence. What happened was a process difficult to explain, but the movements of my body began, and these movements, after a while, no longer seemed to be creating the music—the music, rather, was there, and its insistence was the basis for my actions. This was a state I was familiar with, a state I found erotic. It was a full inhabiting.

When the audience rose at the end, I was, for a moment, terrified. I could not see them because the lights were not yet up, and I did not know, immediately, what they were doing. It was a relief, of course, when they began clapping, but it wasn't entirely soothing. I suspected that even if I'd been terrible, they would still have risen.

They were doing this, really, because of the fulfilment of something. A narrative that had taken over. My return was in many ways the performance.

When the lights finally went up, I could see them all spread before me. They were still smiling, these people, still clapping, but I also noticed how they grew restless; they wanted to leave, to eat, there were other things for them, the performance was one part of a whole day. They would abandon me here. Had I noticed that before? The sense of diminishment even as I stood there, as they clapped and smiled towards me, their hands moving in and out of sequence.

The idea of return becomes foolish. I don't think anyone ever explained this to me properly—what hurt once, hurts always. But I did carry on, anyway. I did succeed in that. They had come to see something, and I had shown them. I began to see failure had never been the correct word to describe what had happened. It had been a cessation, a loss of contact.

The conversation around my return, how the performance engaged with fear, meant the album, the ensuing tour, got a lot of press coverage. I hadn't realised that would be how the music was taken, and neither had the composer. The story felt narrow. The music had been a new thing. It hadn't been entirely unrelated to what had happened to me—I was the one performing it—but that did not mean it was related in any meaningful sense, only how everything is related.

'Aren't most things to do with fear,' the composer said, 'if you poke them enough?'

Billy and I had not spoken since around the time of his show, and the silence between us had begun to feel total. The fact of this was never far from my mind. I was shrouded by this silence. When he emailed, the message felt like a meteor, striking through the surface of my existence. It was long, and from the way the tone changed, how it repeated the same sentiments, sometimes carefully, sometimes more urgently, I suspected he'd written it over the course of a few days, perhaps weeks.

He was happy for me, he said. He was glad I was performing again. He'd seen reviews of the record and had wanted to say something, but he hadn't known how to put things. He told me he'd found it hard when I'd stopped playing, when I'd been unable. He'd hated what it suggested.

I used to like pretending you were always playing for me, always thinking of me onstage (I didn't tell you), but then that happened.

He said he knew, deep down, I blamed him, our relationship, for my breakdown. And it was true that when I'd stopped performing there were parts of him that had enjoyed being needed. Except, then, he said it felt like I went off into a separate corner, so he did the same, and it was like we were both making these tributes with our backs turned to each other.

It was sad. Did you see that? You didn't say.

The message came as if in the middle of a longer conversation, and I realised the silence, for him, had been a pause, not an ending. I was annoyed about the fact he had been able to see it this way. In my reply, I told him they did not feel like tributes. If they were offerings, I did not know what was being offered, or to whom. His sculpture of me hadn't felt like an offering so much as an accusation.

He asked me, then, if it was our relationship, its destruction, that I'd used to return to the cello, and when I told him, yes, he grew bitter. He would not let me have that pain if I was only going to use it.

I waited a while before responding. I knew what he would be facing after his first experience of success: the exposure of his intentions, how wasted they became under the glare of attention. I wondered if this could be the source of his renewed anger. I wanted to explain that the cello was my only safety in the world, which was how I returned to it, but I didn't want to make my desire for it sound childish. It is not childish, though it came to me in childhood. And even though, in part, it is.

Eventually I emailed asking him to meet. I requested he tell me when he was next in London, and, even if I had a performance, I would meet him. When he did not reply, I sent him a text saying he was right that I had always been thinking of him, always playing for him. It had been disruptive.

Billy, it was what I was always trying to tell you.

I travelled for a concert to Yorkshire, and on the train, I read back through our emails, as the carriage emptied, as we got further from London. It was early June. I had entered into an uneasy truce with my panic. I knew that this wouldn't be permanent, so I wanted to know if he thought I should continue performing. I had to know whether it was worth it, to live always at the point of that rupture. It had been a week without a reply to my email, and I tried to call him. When he didn't answer, I considered sending further messages, but I didn't. I knew only a certain number of things could be heard at once before the note of each was diminished.

I booked a flight to Seville without checking if he was there. It was the cheapest flight I could find, which was at six in the morning, and I took a lifeless train to the airport without telling anyone. I went in the dark with only a rucksack, leaving my cello at home in the basement, and on the journey I felt lighter. It had been a long time since I'd travelled without my instrument.

The plane was peaceful. It was almost silent even though it was full of people. Outside the windows, the sun was beginning to ascend, and it silvered the grass to the right-hand side of the runway—the inside of the plane seemed dull in comparison, the flat effect of its strip lighting. Around me people slept, shuffled quietly back and forth in the aisle, adjusted their travel pillows. They rested with the ease of people who knew where they were going. I stared past the sleeping woman to my left, to the dawn exterior and the comings and goings of other planes. I did not know where I was going. It did not feel like the start of a homecoming.

When it arrived, the take-off was sudden. The sound of the engines became so overwhelming that I felt they were inside my own body. As we streaked down the runway, I was reminded of that word *fugue*—Billy's word—and the sense of flight it had left me with. The plane gained momentum, and my back pressed into the seat. I kept my eyes determinedly out the window. I was only afraid for the few moments that followed the wheels lifting from the tarmac.

The entire journey I gazed at the sky and thought of Billy in his studio far below, and then, when we landed, I felt hollow. I hadn't slept, and my neck ached from looking out the window. I bought pastries at a brightly lit café in the terminal where I sat eating them, reading news articles on my phone, as if I was awaiting collection, not grasping anything written. I was delaying the moment I would have to ring him, partly because it was still early, and the earliness of my arrival, I knew, betrayed something of my desperation. Still, I was wary of showing him this. But also, I knew what I'd done was strange, bizarre even.

I ordered more food and wondered about how I was going to explain myself to him. This sort of spontaneity was new to me; I wasn't clear how to present it, or if it would be accepted. I had not come for long, from the size of my rucksack alone that was obvious, so I must only have come to see him. Yet I did not know, I realised, if he would want to see me. He hadn't returned my messages. I wanted to phone someone else, to ask them what I should do, but I knew my friends would find this predicament foolish. They would just tell me to phone him.

I called, and he didn't answer, and I put the phone down on the table. My hands and face became unbearably hot. There were two small girls running around the table next to me, and they kept knocking my chair as they passed, and wherever I moved they kept doing this, and I did not have the language to tell them to stop. Before I could think further, I booked the next flight home, which was that evening, and then sat there eating the sandwich I'd bought, tearing it into tinier and tinier portions. I knew I'd have to treat the day the same as the sandwich, consuming it in manageable pieces, hour by hour, because I was aware that otherwise I might lose myself.

The small girls left, smiling, with their parents, the couples and single people at other tables ate their food absentmindedly, eyes on the departure board. I began laughing, quietly, to myself, more to hear the sound than anything, and I was overcome with relief I'd told no one what I was doing.

I determined that if I kept myself to the inside of the terminal building, it would not be true that I had actually come to Spain, nor failed in my purpose. It would only be true that I had taken a flight and something about that seemed more acceptable. A round trip was a thing of its own, not a half-finished journey. I checked into my evening flight early and then turned off my phone. I did not allow for the chance he might return my call, which surprises me now—how I did not do that.

In the duty free, I bought expensive skincare I didn't need. I lay down and slept on a bank of seats by a glass wall, beyond which planes took off soundlessly. When I woke, I sent an email to the composer on my laptop, telling him I had flown into the airport in Seville only to leave again, explaining how embarrassed I was by this, how in the end I hadn't even told Billy. Then I felt better. The sky was perfectly blue, almost white outside. I knew the strength of the heat, and I was glad to be inside and covered.

I went home. I cried only briefly in a toilet cubicle. I had barely spoken a word in that country, nor left the bounds of the airport. I hadn't gone out to the road that brought taxis and other vehicles. I hadn't stood under the sun for a moment.

The month went by on various stages in front of large and small audiences, where I grew stronger through repetition. Although I knew I had told the wrong person about my flight, it felt easier having done so. The composer found it funny, or at least he decided humour was the best way to approach me.

'People do stuff like that all the time,' he insisted.

Just not so expensive. And the fact of the money mattered because I was trying to move out of my parents' house into my own place. I had gone backward in this. Now, I would have to stay with them longer, in the cocoon of their spare bed.

The composer and I travelled to Berlin for a performance one weekend. The venue was a small music hall, and there was no stage to speak of, nor spotlights. Although I was raised on a podium it did not feel like I was apart from the audience. The composer found performances like this essential. I could see the audience's faces, clearly, and so the box I had fashioned in my mind had to be done away with. I found that rather than playing from a place of intuition—rather than closing my eyes and being seized by the music—I wanted to keep them open. I watched the audience. Whilst some of their faces were impassive, this was not the case for all of them. In fact, I was alarmed by some of their expressions. They seemed wilful, spontaneous. They were not as I'd pictured, and I became more conscious in my performance, fiercer, attempting to correct these expressions, which only became more exaggerated as I did. I wanted to understand why they looked this way. I was alone there, shut out of something, but as I continued, movement began also in the audience—swells of motion, like something was being passed, fluidly, among them. I understood this motion as an answer, a retort, to my own movements, my work, on the stage, and I knew what I was doing. I knew I couldn't undo it, that something had been created.

I was agitated afterwards. It had been so long since I'd felt that connected to an audience that I became slightly manic. I drank with the composer in the bar of the hall, speaking to friends of his, who had their own ideas about what had occurred. The composer spoke of his intentions for the composition and then made light of them, but as much as I listened, I couldn't escape the sense of what had happened. I was riveted by it.

A man in a green linen suit, who was leaning on the bar, began flirting with me, explaining what he'd made of the music, what he'd deduced of me. He was entirely wrong, I thought. I told him this, then we spoke back and forth for a while until I realised although we weren't arguing explicitly, we were involved in a fight. It was where the sense of flirtation was coming from. I considered it was a similar dynamic to the one created during the performance, between myself and the audience, a fight of some kind, a sense of erotic potential. I wasn't clear on who had created it, but I had a strong apprehension, in this, of a self I was inhabiting, and the thing was, I did believe in that self. I wanted to be her.

I stopped speaking to the man because I had no desire for our flirtation to go any further, but the whole evening I hadn't thought of Billy. And there was relief in this, to exist in that place only.

He called just when I was beginning to think I could manage. He'd been in London for a while, he wanted to see me. I thought of myself, sitting alone in the airport. As we spoke, I didn't reveal about Seville, what I'd done, and this seemed connected to what he'd accused me of—that I always had to be certain. Somehow, I knew that not telling him would mean another failure on this point, but on the phone, I couldn't manage it.

I agreed to meet him. We arranged again to meet in Clerkenwell, but this time in a church garden because of the good weather. When I arrived, he was sitting on a bench in a patch of sunshine. He was leaning back, resting, the breeze moving his hair gently. He looked different in a way I couldn't pinpoint. I touched his shoulder, and the fabric of his t-shirt was warm, as if he'd been sitting in the sun for some time, waiting. He stood up to greet me. We embraced for a while, and then we ended up walking, first around the garden before transitioning to the pavements, full of people in suits drinking beers outside pub entrances.

He was more guarded. I saw immediately I might not have to explain some of the ways I'd been feeling because he was probably feeling them too. He was happy with his beginning success, he told me. He was to be included in a bigger show and was selling more pieces and receiving a high amount of interest, also in America, but there was an uneasiness, there was a pressure.

'It's why I went quiet,' he explained. 'I had to get to grips—sort myself out. It was strange.'

He told me again how hurt he'd been by my leaving, to be left alone in that house. The way he explained his feelings, the fact he could, suggested he'd moved slightly beyond them, and I didn't know if this meant he'd moved beyond me. The fact he was there, the way he touched my waist to guide me on whatever route of his mind we were taking through the streets, suggested otherwise.

'I know I didn't consider you there,' he said, finally. 'When I was alone in the house it was like I could see the place more clearly. And it was empty. You were right.'

This was sad, and I wanted to protest it, but he was correct, he hadn't considered me there. He went on to explain that he felt like he'd taken on the role of his father—he'd repeated the pattern of this other man, always dodging, avoiding, whilst at the same time my eventual abandonment had felt the same as that other, earlier, abandonment. I wondered if he thought I'd done that intentionally. I wasn't sure.

We walked through the hot streets, and I listened to him talk and felt us move one way and another as if one body, as if our conversation was being created by the rhythm of our body.

'Was it hard?' he said. 'Being with me?'

This had never been how I'd framed the issue.

'I was just in two places in my head.'

'Not the same place?'

'They didn't feel the same.' I wanted to tell him how they hadn't felt the same, but I didn't know how. 'There was a drop between the two spaces. *They* were true, each of them, but going between them felt like a lie.'

I turned and was glad to find him looking at me.

'Right,' he said.

There came the moment to tell him my uncertainty, how I could no longer tell the right decisions, how I missed him, but in the way that he was looking at me I gathered it might be unnecessary. I didn't need to try and say these things because the way we were walking around the streets without going anywhere, the way we were positioned together, the course we were taking was already telling him. Any failure in understanding was a failure that was inescapable. I said his name, which was enough.

We didn't say much on the bus back. We went silently into the house, so that my parents wouldn't hear us. In the room we were slightly rough with each other, or he was slightly rougher with me, but there was something correct in this. I was glad of it. We fucked and lay in the bed afterwards looking at each other in a way that still wasn't entirely open—a guardedness, I think, which had made the sex so pleasurable. Once again, we were kissing, and an hour or so must've passed before we spoke again.

The afternoon was humid. I went to get us some water and opened the small, barred window onto the street. He told me about the improvements he'd tried and failed to make in his father's house, and then he asked if I'd ever considered coming back, so I told him about flying into the airport. I laughed a little about how foolish, desperate, it had felt. I had expected he might find this funny, but he didn't. It was withholding, he said, it was exactly the problem—me not letting him in, wanting always to be invulnerable.

'Invulnerable?' I repeated, as if I'd never heard of the word. 'But you didn't want to see me.'

'How do you know that?' He was sitting up now. 'I would've liked to be there for you.'

I was amazed by this idea, that somehow asking for help might be a generous or loving action. Although it wasn't clear to me help was exactly what I'd been after, I could see how it might appear that way—at the time, it might've been what I believed. How to explain it? I wasn't sure I'd wanted anything but a chance to experience possibility again. What I'd found instead was erasure—the specific erasure of an airport, an in-between state. To speak to him from there would've been to speak from nowhere, where I feared he wouldn't recognise me, because I would've been no one.

'I wasn't clear about coming back for good, and it would've been confusing.'

'Don't you think it's confusing now?'

'It's been impossible to reach you!'

He narrowed his eyes and in them there was a look, for the first time that day, of persecution.

'Because you left—you just went.'

'You acknowledged, earlier, your part in it.'

'Did you ever want to come back with me?'

From outside the window there came the sound of soft, low laughter.

'Did you think I would?'

He stared at me.

'Of course, I hoped you would.' When I didn't speak, he turned away, and I could hear he was breathless. 'This is fucking torture.'

I said I didn't know how to be in this sort of thing, this sort of love, I just didn't, and then I expected him to present a solution, which of course he couldn't. We broke apart. The communion of our bodies, which had emerged again as if undamaged, could not hold us. In our silence I had an understanding of how if we stayed together, we would eventually come apart in ways like this repeatedly. It seemed to me, then, that love might be a series of islands, which grew further apart as the water took them, as the land on which to stand eroded.

'I've been so lonely,' he said, after a moment.

At some point, later, we dressed. We picked up items of discarded clothing from the floor, without really looking at each other. Our clothes seemed different, creased and misshapen, when we put them back on. Standing in the middle of the room, he said he'd followed the tour, that he'd watched one of the live performances online, and he'd seen enough to know I would continue.

'You watched me?' I said.

He nodded.

He told me there were times he'd been considering our relationship as a thing that would always be unfinished.

'I don't mean it has to be finished,' he said, 'I mean it can't be finished, and maybe now we have to leave it on its own. So, it's still there, but we're not inside it.'

This was the first time the idea of our relationship living on without us occurred to me. He gave me this idea, perhaps because he didn't know what else to do, how to make that moment easier. How to make my decision bearable, and it did feel like my decision. Then he admitted that sometimes it was a relief, not to have to think of me, to be with his work only.

I walked with him away from the house, down the street and towards a junction, where he would catch a bus. He asked me not to wait with him at the stop. After we walked away from each other, down the same long pavement, I turned, and he was stopped at a corner. A summer wind went over us. The traffic lights beside him changed, and it would soon be evening.

I did believe at some point we'd make some move back together, in the way we had before, that something would enable this to happen. Perhaps whatever had previously enabled us. The sense of something unfinished. Yet, we did not. At first, I could barely function, but I had performances to attend, and the routine of these helped, the fact that all I had to do was play my instrument. For long periods of time, I didn't think of him. I was busy being a cellist. When he came back to me, when something brought our memories back, I believed, still, that time was not an agent of separation, that we would find our way back together.

I returned briefly to the quartet, but tensions immediately became so fraught between myself and the lead violinist that I quit again. I moved into a flat with another cellist, and then, a year later, once I was making more money, I moved into my own place. I recorded further albums, both with the composer and on my own. I played at many festivals, in many cities.

Billy and I planned to meet exactly two years after we parted, in Madrid, where I was performing Dvořák's Cello Concerto. He told me he would make the distance, yet as the time grew nearer, things got in the way, both of us had other commitments, he did not think it was a good idea. He was working well—he did not want to ruin his concentration. I remember our last texts then. The concert in Madrid was important, and afterwards he sent me a link with a review, which I'd already seen, but he sent it, and asked *are you happy?* So, I said *yes, thank you,* and he replied, *good—it was worth it, then?*

A few years after I recorded the album with the composer, I was interviewed by a journalist for a national newspaper. She was writing about stage fright and wanted to speak to me about my panic, how it felt to perform in its aftermath.

We met at a café in Central London, which was calm and airy, with surprisingly few other customers. The journalist was sat at a table in the corner, chosen, I assumed, because it provided the greatest sense of privacy. Although that was an illusion, given the nature of our meeting. From the eagerness of her manner, I guessed she was younger than me, but this could also have been due to the roles we occupied around that table. She was recording the meeting on her phone, and she also wrote in a messy looking notebook.

She'd managed to watch a recording of the performance during which I'd had my attack. I'd known about this recording in a vague sense, without realising anyone might ever watch it. She clearly found something surprising in the fact it was something I'd never seen. She asked why I hadn't, which I found an odd question, the answer being obvious: it was embarrassing. She told me it was hard to separate performer from performance, and so much so that whilst watching it, even though she'd realised what she'd been watching was true, I had been having a physical seizure, she couldn't shake the sense I was performing.

'As if the seizure was what you'd actually wanted to do. I hadn't expected that. I had this sense of it being planned and practised.'

I nodded at this because something about the idea of it being intended had always been the thing that I'd found most humiliating, that for several moments many members of the audience would have assumed I was doing something of my own volition. I had not been able to explain it was a mistake, that I'd been powerless. She asked about powerlessness.

'Do you think performance is inherently sacrificial? And do you think that's why so few people can bear to do it?'

I didn't like the word sacrifice because it seemed to hide the amount of selfishness, vanity, that motivates performers. But rather than discuss the mechanisms of stage fright, the different ways in which performers are taught to anticipate and avoid it, she kept on about sacrifice. I asked her to clarify her point,

'Why is sacrifice interesting?'

'Well,' she said, 'I think it's very interesting, to put yourself in that position. But I'm trying to discover the route you took, the way you got better.'

I told her I did not know about that, and if that was the way she was looking at what had happened, she was forcing a narrative. She noted something down and told me she was looking at the nature of performance and panic, she wasn't trying to force anything. She asked some more questions about how it had felt to return to the stage, the work I had done to get there. As she did, I was reminded of the poet in Seville, how her questions did not seem innocent but pointed, revealing something I'd found repellent—a hunger for information that seemed to eradicate experience. I wondered if the journalist was asking the question she really wanted to ask.

I kept having her repeat things, be more specific, and in this I was alarmed to find I sounded like my mother. But it did not seem to me that everything she was talking about was connected. I did not want to concede the path she was creating between a breakdown and a recovery. The fright was always present, it had cost me because it had interrupted a long-held belief. It had rendered a specific viewpoint obsolete, shown how my perspective was always lacking something. She smiled in a tight way, so I knew she found me difficult, prickly, and I wanted to tell her that wasn't all I was, but I resisted the temptation. I was being prickly.

I wondered if what she was really talking about was love, fulfilment, the ways other people want you to be happy, and I realised she might be asking about Billy, but I dismissed the idea as indulgent. My life was small and uninteresting to most, she merely wanted to use me as a vehicle for her own conclusions. But I believed the idea of sacrifice was a lie. It was romance, and I was done, at least, with romance.

In my case, I told her, I wanted to be what I wanted. I was never good at other things, never comfortable in them. It was never one thing over another. Everything else was impossible. In this way, my ability as a cellist, which some might view as noteworthy, was in fact contained within a larger incapacity. A failure, perhaps, of imagination, divergence. A great uncertainty. The idea of recovery was a lie because it had been in my return to the stage that I'd discovered this incapacity. It was why it had hurt me. It was why it was damaging.

As I'd said this, she'd been scribbling words in her notebook, or listening, making little sounds to prove it, nodding. I sounded certain, possibly because of the way her reactions fed into my monologue, solidifying it, but I knew I wasn't.

The other thing I could've said was what she referred to as a recovery actually involved the breakdown of the only other thing I'd ever cared about. Obviously, I didn't say this. Out of curiosity, I asked if she really wanted to speak about my personal life, and she sat up. No, she said, of course not, but then she started smiling, of course, if I wanted, she'd be happy to, she added, with her pen poised.

Over the next few years, I heard about Billy through friends, saw news of his work, exhibitions, had other lovers, forgot him for periods, returned to him suddenly, sent him a text, did not receive an answer, ignored him, was lonely, was occupied. When I considered him, it was often through the distorting effect of my own inabilities.

I had heard he'd been in a relationship with another artist, a painter, and I'd been told conflicting stories about the nature of their commitment, but once they'd been together for a year, I concluded it must be serious. I didn't contact Billy in this time—I could not bear to think of her reading anything I'd written, or to be seen as imposing myself. The idea of her body, the intimacy of their bodies, them together, made me feel without substance, so I didn't think of them. Initially this was easy.

During this period, I gave one of the most celebrated performances of my career, playing Bach's suites in New York. It was not my favourite performance, nor was Bach my favourite composer, but it was received better than I'd believed it could be. In the days after, I remembered playing the same music in Spain years before. The hot, narrow room I'd chosen for myself, the smell of the juniper trees, how sad the music had sounded to Billy. I hadn't been thinking of this before the performance, but I wondered if it had something to do with the quality of my playing, its reception.

Then I heard, through a mutual friend, that the painter was pregnant with Billy's child—although their relationship had broken down. In fact, I was told he'd abandoned this woman when she was six months pregnant, just as they were about to buy a flat together in London, and she had been forced to move in with her sister, where she would raise the child, a daughter. When I first heard this, I didn't believe it. As I heard more, the details seemed to remind me too much of other stories I'd heard, and I began to disregard it further. What stories these were, I couldn't say, but there was a familiarity that I mistook for falseness. I did not believe he would've acted that way.

It was only when he emailed me that my thinking on this changed. He sent me something short and inconsequential, asking how I was, what I was working on, without mentioning anything about his own life, which all seemed strangely breezy. It felt as if he was testing the water, and I decided he must've been seeing if I'd heard anything, and if this was the case, I knew there must have been some truth to the stories. I didn't reply to his email. I resented being tried out like that, but I also had the impression he was asking for something, some help or absolution, and I began to be repelled by my thoughts of him.

The woman was another matter. At this time, I was back in London, spending a week recording an album with a famous vocalist. It had been five years since we'd ended things, since I'd left him, although it still felt as though he had left me. I was in my mid-thirties, and I was childless, which is how I'd always known I would be, and the fact of him having a child did not make me want one, but it did lead me to ask where my certainty had come from. There was something, I felt, contemplating this woman who'd had his child, something that seemed to distinguish us.

I was at the recording studio until very late each evening and when I came home, I would be so wound up from the exertion of recording, I would sit for a few hours drinking a glass of wine in my kitchen. I couldn't get to sleep without doing this, and I enjoyed the stillness, the slow warmth of the liquid, the thought of my empty, waiting bed. I had recently ended a long-distance relationship with a German violinist who would still occasionally phone me during these hours, but mainly I sat at the window looking at the white stone of the church I lived opposite, the lights of a glass tower on the horizon.

One night, I decided to search for this woman online. I had looked her up briefly before to see what she looked like, but I'd always stopped myself from learning much about her, partly because I did not want her to become vivid. That night a light rain was falling soundlessly on the window, and I found information easily. She had given a few interviews to arts blogs and magazines, and there was a video of a talk she gave at an institute, which was shot from diagonally below in a way that seemed amateurish. This talk was something to do with representations of the body, the physicality of her practice, and she spoke well, assuredly, but I was much more interested in watching the movements of her hands as she spoke, the forcefulness of her gestures, how she seemed to be grabbing at the world, or pushing herself further into it.

She had a neat, narrow face and dark features. Her hair was almost black, cut to her pointed chin and, I assumed deliberately, messy. There was a loose fringe that touched her eyelashes. Her arms were bare. She was beautiful in a way that was sexual, uninhibited. Her voice entered my flat through the speakers on my laptop, and I found it playful. I was envious of something about her, perhaps only this sense of play, abandon, even though I knew if someone were to watch videos of me performing, they might make the same assumption, which would only sometimes be accurate and more often would not be.

When I had told my parents about this woman, how she was to have Billy's daughter alone, a singular expression had come over their faces, as they'd looked at me, and I had not been able to put a name to the expression, although it felt recognisable. Some of my friends had made the same expression when I'd told them. It was not quite pity, it was not as simple, or, at least, if it was pity, I was not sure I was the intended recipient. I was not sure who was being pitied, but it could have been both of us: this woman and me, placed together. Yet we were completely different. I was convinced of our difference, watching this video of her—it surged through me. Perhaps a better word than pity to describe that expression might have been unease, but I'm not sure why her life or mine should have put other people at ease. It doesn't seem, at all, a necessary part of living.

As I read more, online, I tried to discover what it was I wanted from this woman. I was trying to find something that might dispel the uncomfortable suspicion that what I wanted of her was only him. That she had taken something permanent from him, and I was jealous, even though I hadn't wanted it, or hadn't wanted it more than other things. What had she wanted? It didn't seem discoverable.

I kept reading, and really there wasn't a huge amount, so I went back and re-read the same interviews, and the sense of our difference, the boundary of it, began to waver. With inspection, under scrutiny, the intentions of her art, her presentation of it, become hazier. She seemed less articulate. My conviction over our differences weakened, not because we seemed the same but because I couldn't hold onto many things about her with certainty. Why did I want difference? I felt it was why I was there. It was what I needed. And it occurred to me I was trying to convince myself he wouldn't have done the same to me, if I had wanted his child, if I had gone about having it, like her, which, really, why shouldn't she have, if it was what she wanted?

I had been putting off looking at her social media, perhaps because I didn't want to be presented with a narrative in which they really had been deeply in love, and he really had abandoned her for no good reason. When I finally did look, the most recent photo was of her pregnancy bump. It didn't show the rest of her body, just the bump and a hint of dark material above and below, under her hip bone.

The photo was not artfully taken, or at least not artful in any obvious way, and it was the first thing of hers that I found effective. It seemed inarguably combative. Directed at him, at everyone who knew the situation: an affront. In the distending of her body, evidence of the distortion to her life that he would not, or could not, take responsibility for. This was what happened, she seemed to be saying. This was how he left me. I looked at this photo of her bare, swollen belly, and I became sick to my stomach.

What I was reminded of at this time, was the sculpture he'd made of me. I recalled going to see it in that crowded gallery, so many years before, and how fearful I'd been, and how Billy had come through the crowd, at one point, to find me. He'd stood before me and asked what I'd thought of the sculpture. Because he did not hug or kiss me, I assumed he'd been observing me before then, but this might also have been a thing of expediency—how nervous he was for an answer. He was excited, too, I could tell from the way he held himself.

'They're very good,' I said. 'They're impressive, shocking.'

'You didn't come over.'

He ran his tongue over his teeth, looked at me, asked again if I thought it was good. He was asking me specifically about the sculpture of me. I told him, yes.

'It is,' I said. 'I didn't come over because you were busy.'

It was good, which is why I'd said it. The fact it was original, the fact I could see how well he'd done what he'd intended, its undeniable presence, how I was proud of him, made the disgust I felt towards it so much harder.

Who was the sculpture for?

That was the question I was left with.

A few weeks later, a friend, a curator, invited me to the private view of an exhibition. She did this offhandedly, assuming I would not come, but I had a day free, and I was curious as to whether Billy might be there—I felt, if he was in London, he could be. The strange excitement, the sense of jealousy, that I'd experienced looking at the painter, had only built. I wanted to know if anything about the stories I'd heard were true. In this way, I'd allowed my feelings for him back in. I'd tricked myself into feeling part of things.

It was with some anticipation, then, that I went to this exhibition. I wanted to see him. I spent some time choosing an outfit, putting on gold jewellery. It was the beginning of spring and I got off the tube early to walk, it was a mild evening, and when I arrived at the gallery, I found my friend, the curator, and discovered I was eager to talk, to listen to her news and emotional dramas. We spoke happily with a few other people there, and the whole time I kept my eyes to the door, scanning the faces for someone I recognised, feeling my heart beating harder as a new crowd entered.

Eventually the curator and I went outside due to the rising heat of the gallery. Also, I felt more comfortable about the prospect of seeing Billy for the first time on the street, before he'd adopted whatever identity he would be required to show inside. I'm not sure if the curator suspected why I was looking around so much, but she asked me about Billy. She knew about the situation, she said, and she wondered if he'd been in touch, if it had upset me. It was shocking, she added, to hear about, quite appalling of him. This word, *appalling*, the moral tone, how it was not a word that had occurred to me in the context of that situation, which seemed far too complex, made me pull a face.

'What?' she said. 'You're ok with what he's doing?'

'I don't think it's so obvious.'

She held my wine glass as I put my long coat on, and she told me she felt it was appalling that men still felt they could abandon women with children and find other women who might come to their defence. I didn't feel like that was what I was doing, but something about the way she was talking made me want to defend him. She asked how I would have felt if he'd done the same to me, and when she said this, I felt myself begin to shake a little. I was incensed, quite suddenly. I told her I'd never wanted children. It was a stupid question. This woman, this painter, had wanted her child, clearly, as there was no suggestion that she was being forced to keep it, and, so, it was her decision. I wanted to know why my friend felt immediately that this painter was a victim, even though, it was how I'd felt, I realised, looking at that photo of her bump a few weeks earlier, like her pregnancy was an affliction.

'I'm not saying she's a victim. I'm saying he should take responsibility.'

'Isn't he allowed not to want children?'

It seemed this was a right that in women was defended. Neither my friend nor I knew the circumstances of how the baby was conceived, if he'd known she wasn't taking contraception, or if the contraception had simply failed, so I didn't know where her stridency came from, her absolutism. Surely, I asked her, she wasn't saying that a man who didn't want children should never have sex. She rolled her eyes. She told me I clearly wasn't over him. She described him and then me as cruel, and I told her she was ignorant.

'You don't always get to do exactly what you want,' she said.

But this seemed obvious. This was, obviously, why I was sympathetic to Billy, who would be facing the truth of that sentiment, reforming his ideas of himself, his life, around it. I asked her if he wasn't allowed a little leeway for that, and she just told me she was shocked I still cared so much.

'I thought you didn't want him?' she said.

I found myself speechless. Sometimes I still felt he was all I wanted. She must've realised she had taken things too far because she asked if I wanted more wine, and I said yes only because I wanted to be alone for a moment. There were a few people standing around smoking on the pavement, but for me the street was entirely empty. I stood watching the corners, knowing I was waiting for him now without even hiding it from myself, and I didn't know why I'd come or why I'd fought his case, or why I so wanted to see him.

*

When I arrived home, the shock of the argument was still with me, and I sat down at my laptop, flushed, to write Billy an email accusing him of everything the curator had. I told him what he was doing was cruel, and it upset me most because I knew he, more than anyone, would be disappointed with himself, which he should be. I wrote this because I was stunned by how much I'd been hurt by my friend's words, how enthralled I still found myself to the idea of him.

Half an hour later, I was composing a text to the curator, when Billy called. I had not expected his reply would come so directly, and my voice was tight when I answered. He asked why I'd just sent that.

'You think I don't know it's selfish?'

'Is it true, then?'

'Why are you asking now?'

'I haven't known what to think.'

'I've never claimed not to be selfish.'

'But you never said you *were*, either.' I said, my voice finally breaking. 'When we were together, I don't remember you making it explicit.'

'Did it have to be?'

I told him it was about incapacity, how I'd blamed myself for what happened, how unusual I'd felt in our relationship. I explained about the argument I'd had with the curator, how painful her words had felt, and was surprised he didn't seem aggrieved to hear people were talking about his situation with the painter. Then I confessed to him I'd been envious, at points, of their relationship, of her ability to be with him.

'It's not exactly worked,' he said.

'Is she speaking to you?'

'Sometimes. She's hurt.'

There was a long silence, which I resisted breaking.

'I've never lied about it,' he said. 'I'm sorry you're upset too. I know it's awful.'

'And your daughter?'

'It was just the last thing I ever wanted.'

He explained he was still in Spain. He'd been going to sell the house, but their relationship had broken down, and he couldn't do it. He'd decided to stay there. It was where he really loved to be. I asked if he was managing to work on anything, and he told me a little about a new project, but he trailed off quickly. He said he'd been spending some time listening to the album I'd recorded of the composer's music, just after we'd broken up, in the evenings, in the garden.

Talking like this, on the phone late at night, the idea of that garden, the home we'd shared, released something between us. We started speaking in ways we hadn't for a long time, and the more we verbalised the more erotic it became, until it was entirely sexual.

I climbed into bed as we did this. After we hung up, it was late, and I was exhausted, and I fell asleep still within the intimacy of that call, the timbre of his voice, the sheets where I'd touched myself, feeling the gratification in my body. It was as if it were a physical thing again, our love, as if he was there with me.

In the days afterwards, I wondered about the selfishness he'd mentioned. I remembered the sense I'd had of our rigidity, how it had made the two of us seem possible, and I considered that I'd used the word *rigid* in place of *selfish* to make it more palatable. What I had wanted to ask was whether his situation had left him with any sympathy for his father. I wasn't able, somehow, to do so. It had felt cruel in the moment. Yet as the days went by, I wished I had asked. He didn't get in touch with me, when I felt it was his place to. So, we didn't speak after that, after such intimacy, which wounded me.

Several months later, in June, I travelled to Milan for a performance. It was new work from an Italian composer, a woman, who was famous in that country, and there was some anticipation about the delivery of this music. The auditorium was busy. I was performing with a young Italian pianist who was already nervous, and there was an issue with moving the piano onstage; the piano lift broke, and at the time we should've been starting, the grand piano was still on the floor with a group of stagehands around it, attempting to manoeuvre its body up the stairs without doing any damage, which seemed impossible.

Several members of the audience, all male, came up to the front suggesting they might help lift the instrument, so that in the end about fifteen people were standing around staring at this thing, some of them pushing it idly, testing its weight.

The young pianist was panic-stricken. If they couldn't get the grand up the stairs, she would be forced to play on an upright. She looked pallid at the thought. I took her away from the frenzy, so that she could get comfortable, at least, with the upright, but after ten minutes one of the organisers came running to find us—after more volunteers had emerged from the audience, the piano had been successfully lifted to the stage.

'It was on the shoulders of twenty men,' he said. 'You've never seen something like it.'

Our start was delayed by a further fifteen minutes because the pianist was so relieved by this, she became momentarily inconsolable.

The success of the performance was aided by the air of achievement already created in the auditorium, which the audience seemed to feel, deservedly, a part of. The mood was festival-like. Afterwards, we went for drinks in the city with the female composer and a few others, including the director of programming at the auditorium, who I'd met previously. He was slightly older, a man with dark curls and a broad smile that I found endearing. When he laughed, his face seemed uncluttered, open. He laughed a lot, and as the night progressed, we seemed to be together often. He became more tactile, at first with caution, but as I returned his touches, his focus on me became more intent. It was welcome. I had finished recording the album that had taken so much out of me, and I was willing for this contact. The city was warm and humming, and the late night was clear, which gave it a sense of abandon.

Subtly, we left the others and walked a few streets over, to another bar, where we found a table. We spoke about our lives quickly over some wine that he'd ordered, and this was done in such a way that it was like coming to an agreement—neither of us was looking for commitment. I needed to be clear about this because I wanted to enjoy myself, and he was the same. After that we stopped talking. We walked to his flat through empty streets where we stopped several times to kiss in doorways. His place was at the top of the building, up many stone stairs on which my heels echoed. It was hot in there, so we opened all the windows and stayed up fucking until the sky became light again, which wasn't after too long, pausing to drink water or eat pieces of fruit that he kept in the fridge.

In the morning, I was woken by the noise of the city's traffic through the open windows. We had sex again in the bright sunlight, and then, as we drank coffee, he said he would walk me back to my hotel via the auditorium, where I could collect my cello. Our agreement still stood, he explained, but he wanted to show me the cathedral.

We left in the same clothes we'd been wearing the night before—he put his suit back on to match my evening dress, so I didn't feel conspicuous. He exchanged a few words in Italian with a neighbour, which were quick and elegant, and I regretted I couldn't speak to him in his own language. I wondered how different our night might've felt to him, speaking in a tongue that was not his. I had no idea where we were in the city, so I followed him, holding his arm from necessity. I found pleasure in this blindness. My dress was silk, and it felt like nothing against my body.

When we arrived at the cathedral, I was shocked by its prickliness. It was gothic, he explained, and all its thin towers bristled—they seemed to be growing, developing, even as we stood there. It was like looking at an emergence. Yet the structure was old, long ago decided. I was curious over this sense, and I wanted to see it better, so we strode across the square, my heels clicking on the paving stones, assuredly, and a number of tourists turned to look at us, dressed up like that, hand in hand, in the cathedral's shadow. I enjoyed them looking. But then when we were in the centre of the square, shielding our faces from the sun, I heard my name called. It was a clear note, unmistakeable, and when I turned it was Billy.

He was standing about ten yards away, staring at me with amazement. He approached, at first gazing at me only, but I saw the moment he took in the man I was with, the director, the thing that disrupted his features. He looked over my long dress and said,

'You must be performing.'

My heels suddenly felt vertiginous. I let go of the director's hand, instantly missing its stability, but I could not hold his hand in front of Billy. I regretted also the thinness of my dress, which I felt might betray the sense I had gathering in my body.

'Yes,' I said, quietly, 'just last night.'

In the silence that followed he studied the director again, this time straightening himself. They exchanged a few words, and then he explained he was on holiday with his mum, who was still in the cathedral.

He considered me, openly, for a moment. I was glad I had at least washed my face before we'd left, but it was bare, and my hair was tangled, and I knew it would be obvious I hadn't slept. Looking at Billy, with the memory of the previous night's abandon, under the heat of the sun, I wanted him desperately. I could tell he felt the same. It was uncomfortable because I respected the director, but it was obvious that something existed between Billy and me. It was for this reason—just as I felt my body moving towards him, the day unravelling, the past returning—that I said we had to leave. He asked if I was sure—he touched my arm and checked I was certain, glancing at the man and then asking in a quieter voice whether we shouldn't talk. We could have dinner together, he said, his mum would regret not seeing me. In the way he did this, I saw how he'd grown older, how he was less hesitant. The collar of his shirt was open, revealing his collarbones, his hair was lighter. He was beautiful. I realised it as if realising it all over again, from the beginning.

I practically dragged the director behind me as we left Billy. *What awful luck*, I kept repeating to this man as we hurried to the protection of a thin street leading off the square. *What fucking luck.* He didn't try to make me slow down, he just told me it was ok, he told me not to worry. Once we'd made it to the street, more like an alley, we slowed down a little, and the director asked who he was, and because there was an understanding between us, and because I was not in a position to contain any of my emotions, I told him something I hadn't meant to.

'He's the only man I was in love with.'

And I put my hand quickly to my mouth, but I could not stop the gasping sound that ended the sentence, nor the tears that came in a hard and desperate way on this man's shoulder, in a Milan alley whilst the tourists pushed passed us. The heat of this crying, the day, how I could smell in the sweat of my body a memory of Billy's scent, our scent together, left me unable to get a grip. The foreignness of the city was bewildering. The man was concerned because I was hysterical, suddenly. I could see he was shaken. I felt ashamed to be so revealed to him. I knew if we ever worked together again this would be what he would think about, the broken sounds I was making in public, as if I didn't realise. As if I didn't hear them.

Eventually, he guided me to a café where I was given some water by the staff, who offered me also a fan and some mints. He told me he knew it would not help, but I did not need to feel worried because he understood, he too had been where I was sitting. I was grateful for this, but my tears would not stop. I could not say anything. Once I'd stopped shaking, he walked me carefully to the road, where we hailed a taxi to the auditorium, and I left him, rudely, at the entrance, racing through the corridors to find my cello. I stayed in the small room where I'd found it, by myself, for about twenty minutes, checking over its body, holding it to me.

The director was still in the lobby when I emerged. I apologised, and then, after he'd made sure I was ok, I left for my hotel where I lay on the large, white bed, unable to produce any more tears, stunned by the strength of the emotion that had overcome me. Everything I had felt the night before seemed vacant. The man was sweet, tender, but he was diminishing with every moment.

I knew I could go to Billy. I knew in this there would be safety, but there would always still be a moment when I would have to leave again, because that state of being, in romance, in love, excluding everything, was one in which I just did not recognise myself. What I had not understood, although in that moment it seemed obvious, was how loss was a process that regenerated itself—an old thing that could become new. Time did not make it gentle. With each regeneration, it became more elaborate. Every time I lost him there seemed more of him to lose.

I booked my room for an extra night and turned my phone off. I wanted to stay there a while longer, where

I didn't know anyone except him, so I could remain, at least, where he knew I was. I drank wine sitting on the balcony, overlooking a beautiful square that was full of streetlights underneath which people strolled and gathered. I drank and felt my body grow restive as the light in the sky faded, and I felt empty, looking down on all of it, but, also, in these moments, I was completely at ease with myself.

I don't know what happened to Billy that day, after I saw him, but he might have experienced some similar upset. Several days later, I had an email from him saying he regretted it, but he didn't think we should speak again. He had wanted to get in touch after what had happened between us that spring, but he felt I'd made myself clear about my desire not to be in a relationship, and he'd wanted to respect that. But he found it too frustrating, the sense of this thing.

He'd thought the idea of it remaining unfinished might be soothing, but it was turning out to be unbearable. He saw there was no reversal in me. He felt, for his own sake, he needed things to be finished. This felt like a blow, and immediately I questioned his version of events. I was in the middle of writing something accusatory back to him, when I re-read his message and realised, after all, it was what I'd concluded. There had been no reversal in me. I did not want a life with romantic love at its centre, and it did not seem possible for our love to exist at the extremities. I deleted what I'd written, and instead wrote, *I know, I agree*. I debated telling him I loved him, but in the end I didn't. After I'd sent the message, I regretted it momentarily, before I became relieved.

I felt, finally, it was over.

There are a series of ambient pieces by William Basinski called *The Disintegration Loops*, which are recordings of a process: he was attempting to digitize a series of tapes, recordings he'd made in the eighties from found sound sources—snatches of noise, really, ambience. As he played the tapes, to re-record them, the loops began to disintegrate. In places, the particles of iron oxide broke from the taping, leaving the plastic exposed, creating corresponding silence on the recording. But he kept going, recording until the loops had entirely disintegrated, and the sound of this decay is what the music is.

The noise of the first loop in particular could be mistaken for the distorted sound of a choir—certainly the effect is of voices, a rising and falling. But it is interrupted by something churning and industrial. It sounds, at times, like the noise of machines–trains, horns, cars–that rise from cities.

In the evenings, I look at the deepening sky and listen to these loops. The gaps, where the music begins to break and unravel, grow longer and longer, so that by the end the sound is only a fragment of its beginning. My mind always fills these blanks in, yet what's lost keeps being lost, over and over. I try to understand that what breaks down may never have been whole to begin with, but often unity is a fantasy I can't relinquish.

The process is letting go, but it's something I can't manage.

A lot of time has passed since that performance in Milan. It was the last time we spoke, although obviously not the last I heard of him. I can't say what he might have seen or heard of me. Recently, I performed at a festival in London, and, after the fact, one of our mutual friends informed me she'd been in the audience, so I was reminded it's possible he's done the same without my knowledge. This idea, of him seeing me perform on the stage, as I believe myself to be, is seductive, but it is a fantasy. Even if he had, I can't say what he would have seen. I doubt it would have been what I wanted.

As time has passed, and I've lost contact with our mutual friends, almost all my information about him comes from what's in the public sphere—from his exhibitions and interviews. I tell myself I've avoided these things, but that must not be right. Possibly I've read a lot. I have never, truly, been without my thoughts of him, if I'm going to admit things. And what's on record, what he makes public, cannot be the whole story. I know this. But each time I see or hear of him, I'm astonished he's moved further into the distance. Because how did that happen? Where did we used to live, and where have we gone to?

In the most recent exhibition of his, the sculptures were different. I would say they were more mature except perhaps what I mean is they were more ambivalent. They were made of wood, this time. In the literature on the walls, in the titles of his pieces, there was talk of things breaking. For the words accompanying one piece he wrote of the will as destructive, yet as I walked between the pieces, peering at the carvings on the wood, their permanence, I realised how fully he'd relinquished the idea of fragility in the physical form, how they would no longer break easily. I told myself repeatedly, as I walked around, I must not touch them, not even one, not even a little, not even to feel the grooves he made, I must not, it was not acceptable. But the urge came from how I could no longer do them damage.

This seemed like a loss again. I feel I should not admit this, should not miss him, should be bolder, more spirited. But I do miss him. I have done so.

I do not know if the will is destructive. I suspect, really, he doesn't either.

At the front of the space, where I'd entered, I stopped under the name *William Lant*, written carefully in slanting, black letters. Around me people entered holding their bags to their torsos, scared of unseen things, and I watched them emerging in the space, circling the pieces, getting closer bit by bit, before getting too close, walking away.

I looked back to that name on the wall and felt, for the first time, I was a person who did not know him.

Should that matter?

It's what I've been asking.

The recording of the performance in which I had my panic attack was done professionally. Unfortunately, the quality is excellent—you can see exactly what happened. It was taken on two cameras, one fixed on me and another on the screens that were displaying the artist's work, which was sliced up in ways that reimagined its original meanings. In the beginning I'm sitting on the stage, and the colours and textures of that work also permeate the stage and the atmosphere of the auditorium. I'm completely still until I begin playing, then it's as if a mechanism has been set running.

I watched this recently. I was wary beforehand, yet I found myself, unexpectedly, laughing after about five minutes. The reason is, I am panicked. It is undeniable. I don't know why anyone let me go onstage because in the video I'm visibly shaking, and it seems bizarre that this was never mentioned, that I was so clearly terrified. My performance is wrong—although the composer was correct that a lot of the audience might not have been able to tell—it is very wrong and from my expression, I know it. I knew what was happening. I wonder if I told anyone, backstage, if they listened. The journalist was right that the panic is so visible it almost doesn't seem to be there, or its being there seems to be the performance.

The attack, when I stop playing, when I throw the instrument from myself, is harder to watch. I find, still, I am unable to trivialise it, even though I know I should. But

I can't bear to see myself alone there. To discard my cello when it shielded me—what madness.

I hate that the recording of this moment exists. The fact that I continued, that I have performed so many times since, doesn't change anything. I want to tell myself this was a good thing, this continuation, the right thing, but I don't know if it matters whether what I did was good or right when it was only living as I could manage. I wanted to perform. I could've done so with Billy, but I wanted to perform more completely. It seems I wanted myself totally even if that totality led to misery, and it has, sometimes, led to misery. But, it hasn't always.

If I could plant the flag of our beginning in more places than one, then I suppose it is true the same could be said for our ending. I don't know if Milan counts as a finish, or that last phone call when we touched ourselves as if we were together. I don't know if we ended when I left Spain for the first or second time, or if we have ended at all—perhaps we ended far earlier, in a moment I can't remember—but there was a last time I saw him, although I resist calling it an ending. It was too fleeting.

It was by the Thames, on the south side, whilst I was walking aimlessly, towards the west, where the sun was. Tourists rode by on red bikes; people ran in bright clothing. It was summer again, a heat wave, and I had just finished a run of performances. I was finding pleasure in walking without purpose. I knew he had an exhibition opening near there, perhaps it was why I had taken that route. I saw him. He was going in the same direction, a few metres ahead, talking to a woman on his left, who was shorter. They did not appear to be lovers. He seemed tired, in the way he held his body, a white paper cup in his hand, which he sipped from occasionally. He drifted from the woman, pulling a leaf from one of the plane trees, dropping it onto the paving stones. His body was still slim, moving between people, careful, in the heart of the city.

I wanted to ask him why he was tired. I wanted to touch his shoulder, find some recognition in his grey eyes, ask him, *Billy, what pains you?* But I had the impression if I called out his name, he might not hear me. His name from my mouth might go nowhere, do nothing. I felt I had no power over the distance between us. Really, all I wanted was to admit that I, too, am lonely.

I suppose it's possible he saw me that day. It's possible he felt also that he might say my name, and then thought better of it. Anyway, it did not happen. We could not reach each other, so be it.

I have lived a long time as a soloist.

What I miss is the life he brought into touching distance: an existence that moved beyond the boundaries I'd set for myself, when briefly it seemed so much was possible. But what I wanted to explain is why I chose this instrument. What is here that keeps me. What intimacy I speak of when I speak of my cello. And I am speaking of intimacy—I am speaking of it even when I am speaking of loneliness. I am speaking of its insistence, how I find myself. I do not know if it is an advantage, this communion, but I could not move from it. I could not take myself even a millimetre. I did not want to. It is something that has been painful. It is something that has been extraordinary. This is the story I can tell.

It shouldn't matter what he'd make of it.

When I woke this morning, early, restless, it was with an idea I should take the strings from my instrument. I have in my possession new strings, which I believe might sound clearer, and it was the sense of this clarity that woke me, startled in the darkness, waiting for the sun and some notion of progression. I do not know for what exactly I was yearning. During sleep, I had touched the foot of some goliath in my mind, but it was gone, receded, and there was only an echo, already dying. I cannot lie that I can bear things fading. I removed each string from my cello, and I replaced them, but I have not yet played the new ones. I have been waiting, wondering what it is I want to hear, what precisely the empty space of this body should be used to amplify. Is it only something new that becomes the expression of sentiments that are old, older than me, older even than this instrument?

Last night I sat with my cello in the back of a large, ornate concert hall, in a small room many corridors distant from the empty stage and the audience, who were watching. They were waiting, and had been for a while, so I was aware there must be a growing impatience for me to come forward.

The organisers did not know where I was, because the venue was massive, and the floorplan was not simple but developed, seemingly, along paths of chaos.

All around they started looking for me.

They were calling out, asking for the cellist, down all the dark corridors.

I heard their little voices coming.

They whispered and chanted with delight, it seemed.

But I could sense their anguish.